W9-DGA-676

BOYLE CO. PUBLIC LIBRARY

3 6402 4000 7139 1

PRAISE FOR PATRICIA HIGHSMITH

"Patricia Highsmith's novels are peerlessly disturbing . . . bad dreams that keep us thrashing for the rest of the night."
—*The New Yorker*

"Murder, in Patricia Highsmith's hands, is made to occur almost as casually as the bumping of a fender or a bout of food poisoning. This downplaying of the dramatic . . . has been much praised, as has the ordinariness of the details with which she depicts the daily lives and mental processes of her psychopaths. Both undoubtedly contribute to the domestication of crime in her fiction, thereby implicating the reader further in the sordid fantasy that is being worked out."
—Robert Towers, *New York Review of Books*

"For eliciting the menace that lurks in familiar surroundings, there's no one like Patricia Highsmith."
—*Time*

"The feeling of menace behind most Highsmith novels, the sense that ideas and attitudes alien to the reasonable everyday ordering of society are suggested, has made many readers uneasy. One closes most of her books with a feeling that the world is more dangerous than one had ever imagined."
—Julian Symons, *New York Times Book Review*

"Mesmerizing . . . not to be recommended for the weak-minded and impressionable."
—*Washington Post Book World*

"A writer who has created a world of her own—a world claustro-phobic and irrational which we enter each time with a sense of personal danger. . . . Miss Highsmith is the poet of apprehension."
—Graham Greene

"Patricia Highsmith is often called a mystery or crime writer, which is a bit like calling Picasso a draftsman."

—*Cleveland Plain Dealer*

"An atmosphere of nameless dread, of unspeakable foreboding, permeates every page of Patricia Highsmith, and there's nothing quite like it."

—*Boston Globe*

"Highsmith's novels skew your sense of literary justice, tilt your internal scales of right and wrong. The ethical order of things in the real world seems less stable [as she] deftly warps the moral sense of her readers."

—*Cleveland Plain Dealer*

"Highsmith writes the verbal equivalent of a drug—easy to consume, darkly euphoric, totally addictive. . . . Highsmith belongs in the moody company of Dostoevsky or Angela Carter."

—*Time Out*

"No one has created psychological suspense more densely and deliciously satisfying."

—*Vogue*

"Highsmith's writing is wicked . . . it puts a spell on you, after which you feel altered, even tainted. . . . A great American writer is back to stay."

—*Entertainment Weekly*

Boyle County Public Library

Slowly, Slowly in the Wind

Patricia Highsmith

W. W. NORTON & COMPANY
NEW YORK LONDON

To Charles Latimer

Copyright © 1972, 1973, 1974, 1976, 1977, and 1979 by Patricia Highsmith
Copyright © 1993 by Diogenes Verlag AG, Zurich
First published as a Norton paperback 2004

This selection of short stories first published in volume form
in Great Britain, by William Heinemann Ltd 1979
First published in the United States of America by
Penzler Books 1985 (Warner Books, Inc.)

All rights reserved
Printed in the United States of America

For information about permission to reproduce selections
from this book, write to Permissions, W. W. Norton & Company, Inc.,
500 Fifth Avenue, New York, NY 10110

Manufacturing by The Courier Companies, Inc.
Production manager: Amanda Morrison

Library of Congress Cataloging-in-Publication Data

Highsmith, Patricia, 1921–
Slowly, slowly in the wind / Patricia Highsmith.
p. cm.
ISBN 0-393-32632-2 (pbk.)
I. Title.
PS3558.I366S6 2004
813'.54—dc22
2004020387

W. W. Norton & Company, Inc.
500 Fifth Avenue, New York, N.Y. 10110
www.wwnorton.com

W. W. Norton & Company Ltd.
Castle House, 75/76 Wells Street, London W1T 3QT

1 2 3 4 5 6 7 8 9 0

CONTENTS

The Man Who Wrote

Books in His Head

E. Taylor Cheever wrote books in his head, never on paper. By the time he died aged sixty-two, he had written fourteen novels and created one hundred and twenty-seven characters, all of whom he, at least, remembered distinctly.

It came about like this: Cheever wrote a novel when he was twenty-three called *The Eternal Challenge* which was rejected by four London publishers. Cheever, then a sub-editor on a Brighton newspaper, showed his manuscript to three or four journalist and critic friends, all of whom said, in quite as brusque a tone it seemed to Cheever as the London publishers' letters, "Characters don't come through . . . dialogue artificial . . . theme is unclear . . . Since you ask me to be frank, may I say I don't think this has a hope of being published even if you work it over . . . Better forget this one and write another . . ." Cheever had spent all his spare time for two years on the novel, and had come near losing the girl he intended to marry, Louise Welldon, because he gave her so little attention. However he did marry Louise just a few weeks after the deluge of negative reports on his novel. It was a far cry from the note of triumph on which he had intended to claim his bride and embark upon marriage.

Cheever had a small private income, and Louise had more. Cheever didn't need a job. He had imagined quitting his newspaper job (on the strength of having his first novel published), writing more novels and book reviews and maybe a column on books for the Brighton newspaper, climbing up from there to the *Times* and *Guardian*. He tried to get in as book critic on the Brighton *Beacon,* but they wouldn't take him on any permanent basis. Besides, Louise wanted to live in London.

They bought a town house in Cheyne Walk and decorated it with furniture and rugs given them by their families. Meanwhile Cheever was thinking about another novel, which he intended to get exactly right before he put a word on paper. So secretive was he, that he did not tell Louise the title or theme or discuss any of the characters with her, though Cheever did get his characters clearly in mind—their backgrounds, motivations, tastes, and appearance down to the color of their eyes. His next book would be definite as to theme, his characters fleshed out, his dialogue spare and telling.

He sat for hours in his study in the Cheyne Walk house, indeed went up after breakfast and stayed until lunchtime, then went back until tea or dinnertime like any other working writer, but at his desk he made hardly a note except an occasional "1877 + 53" and "1939–83," things like that to determine the age or birth year of certain characters. He liked to hum softly to himself while he pondered. His book, which he called *The Spoiler of the Game* (no one else in the world knew the title), took him fourteen months to think out and write in his mind. By that time, Everett Junior had been born. Cheever knew so well where he was going with the book that the whole first page was etched in his mind as if he saw it printed. He knew there would be twelve chapters, and he knew what was in them. He committed whole sequences of dialogue to memory, and could recall them at will. Cheever thought he could type the book out in less than a month. He had a new typewriter, a present from Louise on his last birthday.

"I *am* ready—finally," Cheever said one morning with an unaccustomed air of cheer.

"Oh, splendid, darling!" said Louise. Tactfully she never asked him how his work was going, because she sensed that he didn't like that.

While Cheever was looking over the *Times* and filling his first pipe before going up to work, Louise went out in the garden and cut three yellow roses, which she put into a vase and took up to his room. Then she silently withdrew.

Cheever's study was attractive and comfortable with a generous desk, good lighting, books of reference and dictionaries to hand, a green leather sofa he could take catnaps on if he chose, and a view of the garden. Cheever noticed the roses on the small roller table beside his desk and smiled appreciatively. *Page One, Chapter One,* Cheever thought. The book was to be dedicated to Louise.

To my wife Louise. Simple and clear. *It was on a gray morning in December that Leonard* . . .

He procrastinated, and lit another pipe. He had put a sheet of paper in the typewriter, but this was the title page, and as yet he had written nothing. Suddenly, at 10:15 A.M., he was aware of boredom—oppressive, paralyzing boredom. He knew the book, it was in his mind entirely, and in fact why write it?

The thought of hammering away at the keys for the next many weeks, putting words he already knew onto two hundred and ninety-two pages (so Cheever estimated) dismayed him. He fell onto the green sofa and slept until eleven. He awakened refreshed and with a changed outlook: the book was done, after all, not only done but polished. Why not go on to something else?

An idea for a novel about an orphan in quest of his parents had been in Cheever's mind for nearly four months. He began to think about a novel around it. He sat all day at his desk, humming, staring at the slips of paper, almost all blank, while he rapped the eraser end of a yellow pencil. He was creating.

By the time he had thought out and finished the orphan novel, a long one, his son was five years old.

"I can *write* my books later," Cheever said to Louise. "The important thing is to think them out."

Louise was disappointed, but hid her feelings. "Your father is a *writer*," she said to Everett Junior. "A novelist. Novelists don't have to go to work like other people. They can work at home."

Little Everett was in a day nursery school, and the children had asked him what his father did. By the time Everett was twelve, he understood the situation and found it highly risible, especially when his mother told him his father had written six books. Invisible books. This was when Louise began to change her attitude to Cheever from one of tolerance and laissez-faire to one of respect and admiration. Mainly, consciously, she did this to set an example for Everett. She was conventional enough to believe that if a son lost respect for his father, the son's character and even the household would fall apart.

When Everett was fifteen, he was not amused by his father's work any longer, but ashamed and embarrassed by it when his friends came to visit.

"Novels? . . . Any good? . . . Can I see one?" asked Ronnie Phelps, another fifteen-year-old and a hero of Everett's. That Everett had been able to bring Ronnie home for the Christmas hols was a stupendous coup, and Everett was anxious that everything should go right.

"He's very shy about them," Everett replied. "Keeps 'em in his room, you know."

"Seven novels. Funny I never heard of him. Who's his publisher?"

Everett found himself under such a strain, Ronnie became ill at ease too, and after only three days went down to his family in Kent. Everett refused to eat, almost, and kept to his room where his mother twice found him weeping.

Cheever knew nothing of this. Louise shielded him from every domestic upset, every interruption. But since the holidays stretched ahead nearly a month and Everett was in such a bad state, she gently suggested to Cheever that they take a cruise somewhere, maybe to the Canaries.

At first, Cheever was startled by the idea. He didn't like vacations, didn't need them, he often said. But after twenty-four hours, he decided that a cruise was a good idea. "I can still work," he said.

On the boat, Cheever sat for hours in his deck chair, sometimes with pencil, sometimes not, working on his eighth novel. He never made a note in twelve days, however. Louise, next to him in her chair, could tell when he sighed and closed his eyes that he was taking a breather. Towards the end of the day, he often appeared to be holding a book in his hands and to be thumbing through it, and she knew he was browsing in his past work which he knew by heart.

"Ha-ha," Cheever would laugh softly, when a passage amused him. He would turn to another place, appear to be reading, then murmur, "Um-m. Not bad, not bad."

Everett, whose chair was on the other side of his mother's, would tear himself up grimly and stalk away when his father gave these contented grunts. The cruise was not an entire success for Everett, there being no people his own age except one girl, and Everett announced to his parents and the friendly deck steward that he had no desire whatever to meet her.

But things went better when Everett got to Oxford. At least his attitude towards his father became once more one of amusement. His father had made him quite popular at Oxford, Everett declared. "It's not everyone who's got a living limerick for a father!" he said to his mother. "Shall I recite one I—"

"Please, Everett," said his mother with a coldness that took the grin at once from Everett's face.

In his late fifties, Cheever showed signs of the heart disease which was to kill him. He wrote on as steadily as ever in his head, but his doctor counseled him to cut down on his hours of work, and to nap twice in the day. Louise had explained to the doctor (a new doctor to them, a heart specialist) what kind of work Cheever did.

"He is thinking out a novel," Louise said. "That can be just as tiring as writing one, of course."

"Of course," the doctor agreed.

When the end came for Cheever, Everett was thirty-eight and had two teenaged children of his own. Everett had become a zoologist. Everett and his mother and five or six relatives assembled in the hospital room where Cheever lay under an oxygen tent. Cheever was murmuring something, and Louise bent close to hear.

". . . ashes unto ashes," Cheever was saying. "Stand back! . . . No photographs allowed . . . 'Next to Tennyson?' " This last in a soft high voice. ". . . monument to human imagination . . ."

Everett was also listening. Now his father seemed to be delivering a prepared speech of some kind. A *eulogy,* Everett thought.

". . . tiny corner revered by a grateful people . . . Clunk! . . . Careful!"

Everett suddenly bent forward in a spasm of laughter. "He's burying himself in *Westminster Abbey!*"

"Everett!" said his mother. "Silence!"

"Ha-ha-ha!" Everett's tension exploded in guffaws, and he staggered out of the room and collapsed on a bench in the hall, pressing his lips together in a hopeless effort to control himself. What made it funnier was that the others in the room, except for his mother, didn't understand the situation. They knew his father wrote books in his head, but they didn't appreciate the Poets' Corner bit at all!

After a few moments, Everett sobered himself and walked back into the room. His father was humming, as he had often done while he worked. Was he still working? Everett watched his mother lean low to listen. Was he mistaken, or was it a ghost of *Land of Hope and Glory* that Everett heard coming from the oxygen tent?

It was over. It seemed to Everett, as they filed out of the room, that they should go now to his parents' house for the funeral meats, but no—the funeral had not really taken place yet. His father's powers were truly extraordinary.

Some eight years later, Louise lay dying of pneumonia which had followed flu. Everett was with her in the bedroom of the Cheyne Walk house. His mother was talking about his father, about his never having received the fame and respect due him.

"—until the last," said Louise. "He is buried in Poets' Corner, Everett—mustn't forget that . . ."

"Yes," said Everett, somehow impressed, almost believing it.

"Never room for the wives there, of course—otherwise I could join him," she whispered.

And Everett forbore to tell her she *was* going to join him in the family plot outside Brighton. Or was that true? Could they not find another niche in Poets' Corner? *Brighton,* Everett said to himself as reality started to crumble. *Brighton,* Everett recovered himself. "I'm not so sure," he said. "Maybe it can be arranged, Mummy. We'll see."

She closed her eyes, and a soft smile settled on her lips, the same smile of contentment that Everett had seen on his father's face when he had lain under the oxygen tent.

The Network

The telephone—two Princess telephones, one yellow, one mauve—rang in Fran's small apartment every half hour or so. It rang so often, because Fran now and indeed since about a year was unofficial Mother Superior of the Network.

The Network consisted of a group of friends in New York who mutually bolstered one another's morale by telephoning, by giving constant assurance of friendship and solidarity against the sea of enemies, the nonfriends, the potential thieves, rapists and diddlers. Of course they saw one another frequently too, and many had the house keys of others, so they could do favours such as dog walking, cat feeding, plant watering. The important thing was that they could trust each other. The Network could and had swung a life insurance policy in favor of one of them, against a lot of odds. One of their group could repair hi-fi and television sets. Another was a doctor.

Fran was nothing distinguished, a secretary-accountant, but hers had always been a shoulder to cry on, she was generous with her time, and besides all that, just now she wasn't working, which meant she had more time than ever. Ten months ago she'd had a gall bladder operation, and this had at once been followed by an intestinal adhesion calling for another operation, then her old spinal column trouble (out-of-line disks) had acted up, involving now a back brace which she didn't always wear. Fran was fifty-eight, and not so spry any more at best. She was unmarried and had worked for seventeen years for Consolidated Edison in the subscription (actually the bill-collecting) department. Con Ed were treating her nicely as to disability payments, and they had a good hospitalization plan. Con Ed were keeping her job open for her, and Fran could have gone back to work now, for the past two months even, but she had come to love her leisure. And she loved to be able to answer the telephone when it rang.

"Hello?—Oh, Freddie! How are *you?*" Fran would sit hunched, murmuring softly, as if afraid of being overheard by someone, cradling the lightweight telephone as if it were a little furry animal or perhaps the hand of the friend she was speaking to. "Yeah, I'm all right. You're really all right?"

"Oh, yeah. And you too?" Somehow all the Network had fallen into Fran's habit of doubly verifying that their members were all right. Freddie was a commercial artist with a studio and apartment on West 34th Street.

"Yeah, I'm okay. Say, did you hear those police sirens last night?—No, not fire, police," Fran said.

"What time?"

"Around two in the morning. Boy, they really were after someone last night! Musta been six cars zooming down Seventh. You didn't hear them?" Freddie hadn't and the subject was dropped. Fran murmured on, "Gee, it looks like rain today, and I've gotta go out and do a little shopping . . ."

When they hung up, Fran went on murmuring to herself. "Now where was I? The sweater. Had one rinse, needs one more . . . Garbage has to go to the incinerator . . ." She rinsed the sweater in the bathroom basin, squeezed it, and had just hung it on an inflated rubber hanger on the shower rail, when the telephone rang. Fran lifted the phone in the dressing room, an area between bathroom and dining area, learned that it was Marj (a forty-five-year-old woman who had a very well-paying job at Macy's as buyer) and murmured, "Oh, Marj, hi. Listen, I'm on the dressing room phone, so hang on and I'll take it in the living room."

Fran laid the phone down on the dressing table, and went into the living room, limping and stooping a bit as was her habit since her troubles. Though she was alone now, the habit stuck, she realized, and so much the better, because Con Ed were sending their insurance agent twice a month to snoop and ask how soon she thought she could go back to work. "Hello, Marj, how are you?"

The next telephone call was from a mail order sporting goods store, of which Fran had vaguely heard, on East 42nd Street, offering Fran a job starting Monday in their accounting department at two hundred and ten dollars a week take-home excluding their pensions and hospitalization plans.

Fran experienced a slight shock. How had this place got her name? She wasn't looking for a job. "Thank you. Thank you very much," Fran said gently, "but I'm going back with Con Ed as soon as I'm well enough."

"I believe we're offering you a better salary. Perhaps you could think about it," the smooth female voice went on. "We've filled our quotas, and we'd like a person like you."

Fran's sense of being flattered vanished quickly. Was Con Ed *not* holding her job? Had Con Ed phoned this company to get themselves off the hook of the disability money, which was nearly as much as her Con Ed salary? "Thank you again," Fran said, "but I think I'd prefer to stay with Con Ed. They've been so nice to me."

"Well, if that's your opinion . . ."

When they hung up Fran had a few minutes of uneasiness. She didn't dare phone Con Ed to ask them directly what was cooking. She recollected, thinking hard, the atmosphere of the last visit of the insurance inspector. Unfortunately, she'd forgotten her appointment with him at 4:30 P.M. at her apartment, and the inspector had had to wait nearly an hour for her, and she'd come into her building looking pretty lively in the company of Connie, one of her friends who worked as waitress at night and so had days off sometimes. They'd been to an afternoon film. On seeing the inspector standing in the big lobby (no furniture in the lobby downstairs, because it had all been stolen, even though it had been chained to the wall), Fran had put on a limp and a stoop. She'd told him she thought she was making progress, but she still wasn't capable of an eight-hour-a-day job, five days a week. She'd had to sign her name in a book he had, proving that he had seen her. He was a black, though a nice enough type. He could have been a lot worse, making snide remarks, but this one was polite.

Fran also remembered that that same day she'd run into Harvey Cohen who lived in her building, and Harvey had told her the inspector had accosted him in the hall and asked him what he knew about Miss Covak's state of health. Harvey said he'd "laid it on thick," stating that Miss Covak was still limping, made it to the delicatessen now and then because she had to, living alone, but she didn't look like someone who was ready for a job yet. Good old Harvey, Fran thought. Jews knew how to do things. They were clever. Fran had thanked Harvey profoundly, meaning it.

But now? What the hell had happened? She'd call up Jane Brixton about it. Jane had a head on her shoulders, was more than ten years older than Fran (in fact was a retired schoolteacher), and Fran was always soothed after talking with Jane. Jane lived in a wonderful floor-through apartment on West 11th Street, full of antique furniture.

"Ha, ha," Jane laughed softly, after hearing Fran's story. Fran had told it in such detail, she had even put in the woman's remark that the sporting goods company had filled its quota, and Jane said, "That means they've hired all the blacks they need to and they'd be delighted to stick in a white while they can." Jane spoke with a slightly southern accent, though she was from Pennsylvania.

Fran had been pretty sure the woman's remark had meant that.

"If you don't feel like going to work yet, don't," Jane said. "Life's—"

"As all of us said once, if you remember, I'm only taking money that I've put *in* all these years. Same goes for hospitalization. Say, Jane, I don't suppose you could sign a paper or something saying you gave me a couple of massage treatments for the spine?"

"Well—I'm not qualified, as you know. So I don't see how a paper would count."

"That's true." It had seemed to Fran that one more paper about her physical troubles might add that much more weight to her argument that she wasn't fit for work. "Coming to Marj's party Saturday? I hope so."

"Of course. By the way, my nephew's in town, staying with me. He's my nephew's son, actually, but I call him my nephew. I'm bringing him."

"Your nephew! How old is he? What's his name?"

"Greg Kaspars. He's about twenty-two. From Allentown. Thinks he might work in New York as a furniture designer. Anyway he wants to try his luck."

"How exciting! Nice boy?"

Jane laughed like an elderly aunt. "I think so. Judge for yourself."

They signed off, and Fran sighed, imagining being twenty-two, trying her luck in the great world of New York. She watched a little television on her not very good set. It was an old set, not so big a screen as most these days, but Fran didn't feel like spending the money to buy a new one. The only sharply focused program was awful, some quiz show. All rigged, of course. How could any adult get so excited about winning fifty bucks or even a refrigerator? Fran switched off and went to bed, after lifting off the sofa pillows and its cover and pulling out the heavy metal contraption which unfolded, revealing bedsheets and blankets all ready to crawl into, the pillows being in a semi-circular cavity with an upholstered top which made a decorative projection, even a seat, at one end of the sofa when it was a sofa. She lay thumbing through her latest *National Geographic,* looking at the pictures only because the telephone was still ringing now and then, interrupting her train of thought if she attempted to read an article. Fran's older brother, who was a vet in San Francisco, sent her regularly a subscription to the *National Geographic* as a birthday present.

Fran turned the light out and had just fallen asleep, when the telephone rang. She reached for it in the dark, not in the least annoyed at being awakened.

It was one of the Network called Verie (for Vera), and she announced that she was down in the dumps, really depressed. "I lost my billfold today."

"*What?* How?"

"I was checking out at the supermarket, put it on the counter after I'd paid and got my change—because I was loading my paper bags, y'know—and when I looked again, it was gone. I think the guy behind me—Oh, I don't know."

Fran asked questions fast. No, Verie hadn't seen anyone running away, it hadn't been on the floor, couldn't have fallen behind the counter (unless the checkout girl took it), but it *could* have been the guy just behind her who was one of those people (white) Verie just couldn't describe, because he didn't look especially honest or dishonest, but anyway she'd lost at least seventy dollars. Fran overflowed with sympathy.

"It's good to talk about it, though, y'know?" Fran said gently in the dark." It's the most important thing in life, communication . . . Yeah . . . Yeah . . . It's all that counts, communication. Isn't it true?"

"And the fact that you have friends,"Verie put in, sounding a little weepy.

Fran's heart was touched even more deeply, and she murmured, "Verie, I know it's late, but want to come down? You could stay the night. Bed's big enough. If it'd make you feel—"

"Thanks, I better not. Work tomorrow. Make some more dough."

"You're coming to Marj's party, I hope."

"Oh, sure. Saturday."

"Oh! I talked with Jane. She's bringing her *nephew.* Or the son of her nephew." Fran told Verie everything she knew about him.

It was lovely, Saturday evening, to see all the familiar faces at Marj's. Freddie, Richard,Verie, Helen, Mackie (a big cheerful fellow who was manager of a record shop on Madison and could fix anything electronic) and his wife, Elaine, an equally friendly person with slightly crossed eyes, great to exchange embraces and how-are-yous with people in the flesh. But what made the party special for Fran was the presence of somebody new and young, Jane's nephew. Rather formally, Fran made her way, limping a little, to the end of the bar table where Jane stood talking with a young man in corduroys and a turtleneck sweater. He had dark wavy hair and a faintly amused smile, which Fran thought was probably defensive.

"Hello, Fran. This is Greg," Jane said. "Fran Covak, Greg, one of our gang."

"Howdy do, Fran." Greg stuck out a hand.

"How're you, Greg? So nice to meet a relative of Jane's! How're you liking New York?" Fran asked.

"I been here before."

"Oh, I'm sure you have! But I hear you're thinking about working here." Fran's mind was suddenly racing over people she knew who might be of help to Greg. Richard, who was a designer but more for theater. Marj, who might know someone in Macy's furniture department who might put Greg onto someone who—

"Fran! How's my girl!" Jeremy's arm encircled Fran's trouser-suited waist, and he slapped her playfully on the behind. Jeremy was about fifty-five with a shock of white hair.

"Jeremy! You're looking marvelous!" Fran said. "Love that crazy purple shirt!"

"How's the spine?" Jeremy asked.

"Better, thanks. Takes time. Have you met Greg yet? Jane's nephew."

Jeremy hadn't, and Fran introduced them. "What're your job plans, Greg?" Fran asked.

"I don't want to talk about work tonight," Greg replied, smiling and evasive.

"It's just that I was thinking," Fran went on to Jane in her earnest, clear way, though she spoke as gently as she spoke into her telephone, "among all the people we know, we'll certainly be able to do something for Greg. Give him the right ontrays, y'know? Jane says you're a furniture designer, Greg."

"Yeah, well. If you want me to go into my life story, I've been working for a cabinetmaker more than a year now. All handmade

Boyle County Public Library

stuff, so naturally I designed a few things while I was there. Cabinets to certain specifications."

Fran glanced at his hands and said, "Bet you're strong. Isn't he a nice boy, Jeremy?"

Jeremy nodded and tossed back his scotch on the rocks.

Jane said, "Don't worry about Greg. I'll talk to Marj maybe in the course of the evening."

Fran brightened. "That's just what I'd been thinking! Someone at Macy's—"

"I don't want to work at Macy's," Greg said pleasantly but firmly. "I'm rather the independent type."

Fran gave him a motherly smile. "We don't mean for you to *work* at Macy's. Leave it to us."

There was a little music and dancing around eleven, but not so much noise that the neighbors might complain. Marj lived on the fourteenth floor (really the thirteenth) of a rather swank apartment house in the East Forties with round-the-clock doormen. Fran had only a 4 P.M. till midnight doorman, which meant it wasn't one hundred percent safe for her to arrive home after midnight, when she would have to use her downstairs key to get into her building. Thinking of this reminded her of Susie, whom she hadn't seen since her awful experience in the East Village about three weeks ago.

Fran found Susie, a tall, good-looking woman of about thirty-four, sitting on a double bed in an adjoining room, talking with Richard and Verie. Fran had first to say a few words to Verie, of course, about her billfold.

"I'd rather forget it," Verie said. "Part of the game. And the game's a rat race. We're surrounded by rats."

"Hear, hear!" said Richard. "But not everybody's a rat. There's always *us!*"

"That's right!" said Fran, feeling mellow now because she seldom drank alcohol, and what she had drunk was warming the cockles. "I was saying to Verie the other night, the most important thing in life is to communicate with people you love. Isn't it true?"

"True," said Richard.

"Y'know, when Verie called me up about her billfold—" Fran realized no one was listening, so she addressed Susie directly. "Susie, darling, are *you* recovering? Y'know, I haven't seen you since that thing in the East Village, but I heard about it." Of all the Network, Susie perhaps telephoned the least, and Fran hadn't even been treated to a firsthand account. It was Verie and Jeremy who'd filled Fran in.

"Oh, I'm all right," Susie said. "They thought my nose was broken, but it wasn't. Just this shaved spot on my head, and you can hardly see it now because it's growing out." Susie tipped her well-groomed head towards Fran so that Fran could see the shaved spot, nearly concealed, it was true, by billows of reddish-brown hair.

A pang went through Fran. "How many stitches?"

"Eight, I think," Susie said, smiling.

Susie and a friend, whom Susie had driven home in her, Susie's, car, had been attacked by a tall black as soon as Susie's friend had pulled out her front door key. They'd been trapped then between the outside door and the main locked door, the black had taken their money, wristwatches and rings ("Luckily the rings came off," Fran remembered Jeremy reporting Susie as having said, "because some of them cut your fingers off if they can't get the rings off, and this fellow had a knife"), and then the black had told them both to get down on the floor for raping purposes, but meanwhile Susie, who was pretty tall, had been putting up a hell of a fight and wasn't about to get down on the floor. The other girl screamed, someone who lived in the building finally heard them, and yelled back that he was going to call the police, whereupon the black ("maybe thinking the jig was up," Jeremy had said) pulled out some heavy instrument and whammed Susie over the head with it. Blood had spurted all over the walls and ceiling, and this was what had necessitated the stitches. Fran was thrilled that one of *them* had put up a real fight, unarmed, against the barbarians.

"Something I'd rather forget," Susie said to Fran's wondering face. "I'm going to judo classes now, though. After all, we've got to live here."

"But nobody has to live in the *East Village,*" Fran said. "They've got everything there, y'know, blacks, Puerto Ricans, spicks, just name it. You don't see anybody *home* there late at night!"

By this time the big baked ham, the roast beef and potato salad on the buffet table had been well explored. Fran felt mellower than ever, sitting on a bed in one of Marj's two bedrooms (what elegance!) with several of the Network. They were talking about New York, what kept them here, besides the money. Richard was from Omaha, Jeremy from Boston. Fran had been born on Seventh Avenue and 53rd Street. "Before all those high buildings went up," Fran said. She considered her birthplace (now an office building) the heart of the city, though of course there could be other hearts of the city, if one thought about it: West 11th Street, Gramercy Park, even Yorkville. New York was exciting and dangerous, always changing—for the worse and for the better. Even Europe had to admit that New York was the art center of the world now. It was just too bad that the high welfare payments attracted the worst of America, not always black or Puerto Rican by any means, just people who wanted to sponge. America's intentions were good. Just look at the Constitution that could stand up to anything, even Nixon, and come out winning. There was no doubt that America had *started out* right . . .

When Fran woke up the next morning, she didn't remember much about getting home, except she was sure that good old Susie had driven her home in her Cadillac (Susie was a model and made good money) and Fran thought Verie had been in the car too. Fran found in a pocket of her suit jacket, which she had not hung up last night, only put on the back of a chair, a note. "Fran dear, will call Carl at Tricolor in regard to Greg, so don't worry. Have told Jane. Love, Richard."

Wasn't that nice of Richard! "I knew he'd come up with something," Fran said softly to herself, smiling.

The telephone rang. Fran moved towards it, still in pajamas, and noticed by the clock on the coffee table that it was twenty past nine. "H'lo?" Fran murmured.

"Hi, dear, it's Jane. Greg can bring the pot roast up around eleven. All right?"

"Oh sure, I'll be here. Thanks, Jane." Fran vaguely remembered the promise of a pot roast. People were still giving her things to eat, as they had in her worst days when she'd been too incapacitated for shopping. "I thought Greg was awfully nice. He's really got character."

"He's seeing a friend of Richard's later this morning."

"Tricolor. I know. I'll keep my fingers crossed."

"Marj wants him to meet someone too. Nothing to do with Macy's proper, as I understand it," Jane said.

They talked for another few minutes, going over the party, and when she had hung up, Fran made some instant coffee and orange juice from a frozen tin. She folded her bed away, got dressed, all the while murmuring to herself such things as, "Did I take those arthritis pills yet? No, must do that . . . Tidy up a little. No, I suppose the place doesn't look bad . . ." And of course the telephone rang two or three times, delaying all these activities, so the next thing she knew there was a ring from downstairs, and Fran saw it was five past eleven.

Fran assumed it was Greg and pushed the release button. She hadn't a speaker through which she could talk to downstairs. When her apartment doorbell rang, Fran peeked through the round hole in the door and saw that it was Greg.

"Greg?"

"It's me," Greg said.

Fran opened the door.

Greg was carrying a heavy red casserole with a lid. "Jane said she wanted to leave it in this so you'd get all the juice."

"Just lovely, Greg. Thank you!" Fran said, taking it. "Your aunt Jane makes the most wonderful pot roasts, marinates them overnight, you know?" Fran deposited the casserole in her narrow kitchen. "Sit down, Greg. Would you like a cup of coffee?"

"No, thanks. I have a date in a few minutes." Greg wandered around the living room, looking at everything, wringing his hands.

"I wish you luck today, Greg. I offered to put you up, you know. I told Jane. Sounds ridiculous because she's got a bigger place. But if ever you're in this neck of the woods, I have a friend nearby I could stay with overnight. You could stay here. No trouble at all."

"I wish all of you wouldn't treat me like a kid," Greg said. "I'm going to take a furnished room. I like to be on my own."

"I understand. It's *normal*." But Fran didn't really understand. Separating himself from his *friends* like that? "I don't consider you a child, honestly!"

"It's enough to smother anybody. I hope you don't think I'm rude, saying that. It's like a clique—I mean the group last night."

Fran's polite, self-protective smile spread. She almost said, *All right, try it on your own,* but controlled herself for which she felt rather well-behaved and superior. "I know. You're a big boy."

"Not even a boy. I'm grown up." Greg nodded by way of affirmation or farewell, and went to the door. "Bye-bye, Fran, and I hope the roast is good."

"Luck, Greg!" she called after him, and heard him taking the stairs down. Six flights, there were.

Two days passed. Fran rang Jane to ask how Greg was doing. Jane chuckled. "Not too well. He moved out—"

"Yes, he told me he was going to." Fran had of course telephoned Jane to say how good the pot roast was, but she hadn't mentioned Greg's saying he was going to move.

"Well, he got rolled the same night, night before last."

"Rolled?" Fran was horrified. "Was he hurt?"

"No, luckily. It was—"

"Where'd it happen?"

"Around Twenty-third and Third around one A.M. Greg said. He'd just come out of one of those bars that serve breakfast. I know he wasn't tight, because he hardly drinks even beer. Well, as he was walking to where his room is—"

"Where is his room?"

"Somewhere on East Nineteenth. Two fellows jumped on him and pulled his jacket up over his head, you know, sat him down the way they do elderly people on the sidewalk, and took what money he had. Fortunately he had only about twelve dollars on him, he said." Jane laughed softly again.

But Fran was pained deep within herself, as if the humiliating, sordid event had happened to a member of her own family. "The best thing is, if it teaches him a lesson. He can't walk the streets alone that late at night, even if he is young and strong."

"He said he fought back. He's got bruised ribs for his pains. But the worst is, he refused to see the man Marj wanted him to meet, another buyer who knows all kinds of cabinetmakers. Greg could've got some well-paying—finishing jobs at least."

It was unbelievable to Fran. "He's headed for failure," Fran announced solemnly.

Fran telephoned Jeremy to tell him about Greg. Jeremy was as surprised as Fran that Greg hadn't followed up Marj's introduction.

"Boy's got a lot to learn," Jeremy said. "Good thing he had just a few dollars on him this time. Maybe it won't happen again, if he's careful."

Fran assured Jeremy that that was what she'd told Jane. Fran's heart, unfulfilled by maternity, was suffering the most awful perturbations since Jane's news.

"I know a couple of painters in SoHo," Jeremy said. "I'm

going to try there, ask if they need any cabinet work done. You know where I can reach Greg if I come up with something?"

"No, but I'm sure Jane'll know. He's somewhere on East Nineteenth Street."

A few minutes later, when they had hung up, Fran went out and walked a couple of blocks in order to deposit her disability check at her bank and to pick up a few things at the delicatessen supermarket downstairs, and when she got back, the telephone was ringing. She just made it before it logically should have stopped ringing, she thought, and found that it was Richard.

"The Tricolor people didn't have anything for Greg," Richard said. "I'm sorry about that, but I'll think of something else. How's he doing? Have you heard?"

Fran filled him in. She lit a cigarette and spoke long into the yellow telephone by the sofa, expressing her philosophy of no stone unturned, of not trying to be bigger than you really were. "I don't mean Greg's swellheaded. He's just so immature . . ." What she meant was that he *had* to come under their collective wing, that they mustn't let him escape, or rather fly away, to certain doom. "Maybe you should talk to him, Richard, man to man, you know? Maybe he'd listen, more than he listens to Jane."

On Friday, when Fran's cleaning woman came to do two hours in the apartment, Fran made a date to return Jane's iron casserole. Fran loved Jane's apartment on West 11th. Jane had nice, knobby furniture always shining with polish, lots of books, and a real fireplace. Jane had made tea, and said something about spiking the second cup with vodka if they felt so inclined. When Fran asked how Greg was, Jane lifted a finger to her lips.

"Sh-h, he's in there," Jane whispered, pointing towards a bedroom door.

"Is he all right?"

"He's a little shook up. I don't think he wants to see anybody," Jane said with a quiet smile. Jane explained that just last night when Greg had gone back to his place after a late movie, he had found that his room had been broken into and everything stolen, his portable typewriter, his clothes, shoes, everything.

"How awful!" Fran whispered, leaning forward.

"I think what hurt him the most is losing his stud box with his father's cufflinks. My nephew—Greg's father—died two years ago, you know. And a ring or something that his girl friend in Allentown gave him. Greg's having a bad day."

"Oh, I can understand—"

"It's a shame, because I'd suggested that he leave anything valuable here with me, you know. This house has never had a robbery, knock wood." Jane did so.

"Does he—What does he want to do now?"

"He'll try again, I know. He's bloodied but unbowed."

"We've just got to help him."

Jane said nothing, but Fran could see that she was thinking too. Jane went and got the vodka bottle.

"I think the sun's sufficiently over the yardarm," Jane said.

How nice it was, Fran thought, to have friends like Jane.

The telephone rang. It was near the fireplace, and Fran could hear Jeremy's slightly husky voice asking Jane if she knew how he could reach Greg.

"He's here, but I think he's asleep. He's had a tough day. Can I take a message?"

Then Jeremy talked, Jane took a pencil, and she smiled. "Thanks so much, Jeremy. That does sound—rather ideal. I'll tell him as soon as he wakes up." When she had hung up, she said to Fran, "Jeremy found out that Paul Ridley in SoHo needs a lot of shelves put up right away—along a whole wall. You know how big those studios are down there. Sounds like Greg's dish."

"Good old Jeremy!"

"And Ridley—he's tops now. I bet it'll lead to other things—freelance. That's the way Greg wants to work."

"Let's hope he doesn't turn it down just because it came from *us*," Fran murmured.

"Ha! Maybe he's learned something. All the young have to learn." Jane swept her long, straight, graying hair back from her face and picked up her vodka.

Fran felt suddenly—civilized. That was the only word she could find for it. And strong. And solid. All because of people like Jane, all because of *communicating*. Fran went home in a glow. She took the bus up Eighth. The subway rattled just below the pavement outside her apartment building, a subway entrance was right there, but Fran never took the subway anymore. Buses were cleaner and safer, and often she bought "day excursions" as she and her friends called them, a ticket for three rides for seventy cents instead of a dollar ten, if you used it from 10 A.M. to 4 P.M., not in the rush hours. And one day a week the Museum of Modern Art was free, all you had to do was make a contribution, pay what you felt like, or pay nothing. Fran forced herself to wait two days before she telephoned Jane to ask how Greg had made out.

"My dear, it couldn't be better," Jane said in her drawling way. "He's got work lined up for the next six weeks and he's happy as a clam. He likes the informality down there. And I think the SoHo people like him too."

Fran smiled. "Tell him—Jane, you gotta give him my congratulations, would you? I don't care if he doesn't want my congratulations, tell him anyway." Fran laughed with joy.

The happy news about Greg even made Fran feel unworried and quite confident about the visit from the black Columbia Fire Insurance inspector due tomorrow morning at eleven. He worked for Columbia Fire, but Con Ed apparently employed Columbia Fire. Greg's success had given Fran a big charge of self-assurance.

Fran put on her limp the next morning, and admitted the black inspector to her clean and tidy apartment, even gave him a cup of coffee.

"Takes time," Fran said, "but the doctor says I'm doing as well as can be expected. Believe me, I'll tell Con Ed when I feel up to working again. It's not much fun doing nothing day after day."

Work with the system, Fran was thinking. Don't try to buck it, let it work for you. All the money she was getting she'd put *in* in the past, so why not use it now, because how did she know she'd even be alive by the time—

"Okay, Miss Covak, could you sign this please? Then I'll be on my way—Glad you're feeling better."

What a relief—to be alone again! The phone rang. Verie. She told Verie about Greg. Then Fran cleared out and tidied her chest of drawers, which she'd meant to do for months. At 6 P.M. her doorbell rang, and Fran saw through the peephole that it was Buddy, her doorman, in visored cap and shirtsleeves as usual.

"Flowers, Miss Covak."

Fran opened the door. "Flowers?"

"Tha's right. Just delivered downstairs. Thought I'd bring 'em up. Got a birthday?"

"No." Fran was fussing around in the pockets of her coats in the front closet, looking for fifty cents to give Buddy. She found two quarters. "Thank you, Buddy. Aren't they pretty?" She could see pink blossoms through the green tissue.

"Bye now," said Buddy.

With the flowers was a small envelope with a note in it. Fran saw it was signed by Greg before she read the message. It said: "Sorry I was a little abrupt. Sure appreciate your kindness. Also of your friends. Best, Greg."

Fran hastened to get the long-stemmed gladioli into the tallest vase she had, set them on her glass-topped coffee table in front of the sofa, then made for the telephone to call Jeremy.

Fran said, "Jeremy! I think Greg's one of *us* now . . . Yeah, isn't it great?"

The Pond

Elinor Sievert stood looking down at the pond. She was half thinking, half dreaming, or imagining. Was it safe? For Chris? The agent had said it was four feet deep. It was certainly full of weeds, its surface nearly covered with algae or whatever they called the little oval green things that floated. Well, four feet was enough to drown a four-year-old. She must warn Chris.

She lifted her head and walked back towards the white, two-story house. She had just rented the house, and had been here only since yesterday. She hadn't entirely unpacked. Hadn't the agent said something about draining the pond, that it wouldn't be too difficult or expensive? Was there a spring under it? Elinor hoped not, because she'd taken the house for six months.

It was two in the afternoon, and Chris was having his nap. There were more kitchen cartons to unpack, also the record player in its neat, taped carton. Elinor fished the record player out, connected it, and chose an LP of New Orleans jazz to pick her up. She hoisted another load of dishes up to the long drainboard.

The doorbell rang.

Elinor was confronted by the smiling face of a woman about her own age.

"Hello. I'm Jane Caldwell—one of your neighbors. I just wanted to say hello and welcome. We're friends with Jimmy Adams, the agent, and he told us you'd moved in here."

"Yes. My name's Elinor Sievert. Won't you come in?" Elinor held the door wider. "I'm not quite unpacked as yet—but at least we could have a cup of coffee in the kitchen."

Within a few minutes, they were sitting on opposite sides of the wooden table, cups of instant coffee before them. Jane said she had two children, a boy and a girl, the girl just starting school, and that her husband was an architect and worked in Hartford.

"What brought you to Luddington?" Jane asked.

"I needed a change—from New York. I'm a freelance journalist, so I thought I'd try a few months in the country. At least I call this the country, compared to New York."

"I can understand that. I heard about your husband," Jane said on a more serious note. "I'm sorry. Especially since you have a small son. I want you to know we're a friendly batch around here, and at the same time we'll let you alone, if that's what you want. But consider Ed and me neighbors, and if you need something, just call on us."

"Thank you," Elinor said. She remembered that she'd told Adams that her husband had recently died, because Adams had asked if her husband would be living with her. Now Jane was ready to go, not having finished her coffee.

"I know you've got things to do, so I don't want to take any more of your time," said Jane. She had rosy cheeks, chestnut hair. "I'll give you Ed's business card, but it's got our home number on it too. If you want to ask any kind of question, just call us. We've been here six years—Where's your little boy?"

"He's—"

As if on cue, Chris called, "Mommy!" from the top of the stairs.

Elinor jumped up. "Come down, Chris! Meet a nice new neighbor!"

Chris came down the stairs a bit timidly, holding on to the banister.

Jane stood beside Elinor at the foot of the staircase. "Hello, Chris. My name's Jane. How are you?"

Chris's blue eyes examined her seriously. "Hello."

Elinor smiled. "I think he just woke up and doesn't know where he is. Say 'How do you do,' Chris."

"How do you do," said Chris.

"Hope you'll like it here, Chris," Jane said. "I want you to meet my boy Bill. He's just your age. Bye-bye, Elinor. Bye, Chris!" Jane went out the front door.

Elinor gave Chris his glass of milk and his treat—today a bowl of apple sauce. Elinor was against chocolate cupcakes every afternoon, though Chris at the moment thought they were the greatest things ever invented. "Wasn't she nice? Jane?" Elinor said, finishing her coffee.

"Who is she?"

"One of our new neighbors." Elinor continued her unpacking. Her article-in-progress was about self-help with legal problems. She would need to go to the Hartford library, which had a newspaper department, for more research. Hartford was only a half hour away. Elinor had bought a good secondhand car. Maybe Jane would know a girl who could baby-sit now and then. "Isn't it nicer here than in New York?"

Chris lifted his blond head. "I want to go outside."

"But of course! It's so sunny, you won't need a sweater. We've got a garden, Chris! We can plant—radishes, for instance." She remembered planting radishes in her grandmother's garden when she was small, remembered the joy of pulling up the fat red and white edible roots. "Come on, Chris." She took his hand.

Chris's slight frown went away, and he gripped his mother's hand.

Elinor looked at the garden with different eyes, Chris's eyes. Plainly no one had tended it for months. There were big prickly weeds between the jonquils that were beginning to open, and the peonies hadn't been cut last year. But there was an apple tree big enough for Chris to climb in.

"Our garden," Elinor said. "Nice and sloppy. All yours to play in, Chris, and the summer's just beginning."

"How big is this?" Chris asked. He had broken away and was stooped by the pond.

Elinor knew he meant how deep was it. "I don't know. Not very deep. But don't go wading. It's not like the seashore with sand. It's all muddy there." Elinor spoke quickly. Anxiety had struck her like a physical pain. Was she still reliving the impact of Cliff's plane against the mountainside—that mountain in Yugoslavia that she'd never see? She'd seen two or three newspaper photographs of it, blotchy black and white chaos, indicating, so the print underneath said, the wreckage of the airliner on which there had been no survivors of one hundred and seven passengers plus eight crewmen and stewardesses. No survivors. And Cliff among them. Elinor had always thought air crashes happened to strangers, never to anyone you knew, never even to a friend of a friend. Suddenly it had been Cliff, on an ordinary flight from Ankara. He'd been to Ankara at least seven times before.

"Is that a snake? Look, Mommy!" Chris yelled, leaning forward as he spoke. One foot sank, his arms shot forward for balance, and suddenly he was in water up to his hips. "Ugh! Ha-ha!" He rolled sideways on the muddy edge, and squirmed backward up to the level of the lawn before his mother could reach him.

Elinor set him on his feet. "Chris, I told you not to try wading! Now you'll need a bath. You see?"

"No, I won't!" Chris yelled, laughing, and ran off across the grass, bare legs and sandals flying, as if the muddy damp on his shorts had given him a special charge.

Elinor had to smile. Such energy! She looked down at the pond. The brown and black mud swirled, stirring long tentacles of vines, making the algae undulate. It was a good seven feet in diameter, the pond. A vine had clung to Chris's ankle as she'd pulled him up. Nasty! The vines were even growing out onto the grass to a length of three feet or more.

Before 5 P.M., Elinor rang the rental agent. She asked if it would be all right with the house-owner if she had the pond drained. Price wasn't of much concern to her, but she didn't tell Mr. Adams that.

"It might seep up again," said Mr. Adams. "The land's pretty low. Especially when it rains and—"

"I really don't mind trying it. It might help," Elinor said. "You know how it is with a small child. I have the feeling it isn't quite safe."

Mr. Adams said he would telephone a company tomorrow morning. "Even this afternoon, if I can reach them."

Mr. Adams telephoned back in ten minutes and told Elinor that the workmen would arrive the next morning, probably quite early.

The workmen came at 8 A.M. After speaking with the two men, Elinor took Chris with her in the car to the library in Hartford. She deposited Chris in the children's book section, and told the woman in charge there that she would be back in an hour for Chris, and in case he got restless, she would be in the newspaper archives.

When she and Chris got back home, the pond was empty but muddy. If anything, it looked worse, uglier. It was a crater of wet mud laced with green vines, some as thick as a cigarette. The depression in the garden was hardly four feet deep. But how deep was the mud?

"I'm sorry," said Chris, gazing down.

Elinor laughed. "Sorry?—The pond's not the only thing to play with. Look at the trees we've got! What about the seeds we bought? What do you say we clear a patch and plant some carrots and radishes—now."

Elinor changed into blue jeans. The clearing of weeds and the planting took longer than she had thought it would, nearly two hours. She worked with a fork and a trowel, both a bit rusty, which she'd found in the toolshed behind the house. Chris drew a bucket of water from the outside faucet and lugged it over, but while she and Chris were putting the seeds carefully in, one inch deep, a roll of thunder crossed the heavens. The sun had vanished. Within seconds, rain was pelting down, big drops that made them run for the house.

"Isn't that wonderful? Look!" Elinor held Chris up so he could see out of a kitchen window. "We don't need to water our seeds. Nature's doing it for us."

"Who's nature?"

Elinor smiled, tired now. "Nature rules everything. Nature knows best. The garden's going to look fresh and new tomorrow."

The following morning, the garden did look rejuvenated, the grass greener, the scraggly rose bushes more erect. The sun was shining again. And Elinor had her first letter. It was from Cliff's mother in Evanston. It said:

Dearest Elinor,

We both hope you are feeling more cheerful in your Connecticut house. Do drop us a line or telephone us when you find the time, but we know you are busy getting settled, not to mention getting back to your own work. We send you all good wishes for success with your next articles, and you must keep us posted.

The Polaroid shots of Chris in his bath are a joy to us! You mustn't say he looks more like Cliff than you. He looks like both of you . . .

The letter lifted Elinor's spirits. She went out to see if the carrot and radish seeds had been beaten to the surface by the rain—in which case she meant to push them down again if she could see them—but the first thing that caught her eye was Chris, stooped again by the pond and poking at something with a stick. And the second thing she noticed was that the pond was full again. Almost as high as ever! Well, naturally, because of the hard rain. Or was it natural? It had to be. Maybe there was a spring below. Anyway, she thought, why should she pay for the draining if it didn't stay drained? She'd have to ring the company today. Miller Brothers, it was called.

"Chris? What're you up to?"

"Frog!" he yelled back. "I *think* I saw a frog."

"Well, don't try to catch it!" Damn the weeds! They were back in full force, as if the brief draining had done them good. Elinor went to the toolshed. She thought she remembered seeing a pair of hedge clippers on the cement floor there.

Elinor found the clippers, rusted, and though she was eager to attack the vines, she forced herself to go to the kitchen first and put a couple of drops of salad oil on the center screw of the clippers. Then she went out and started on the long, grapevine-like stems. The clippers were dull, but better than nothing, faster than scissors.

"What're you doing that for?" Chris asked.

"They're nasty *things*," Elinor said. "Clogging the pond. We don't want a messy pond, do we?" *Whack-whack!* Elinor's espadrilles sank into the wet bank. What on earth did the owners, or the former tenants, use the pond for? Goldfish? Ducks?

A carp, Elinor thought suddenly. If the pond was going to stay a pond, then a carp was the thing to clean it, nibble at some of the vegetation. She'd buy one.

"If you ever fall in, Chris—"

"What?" Chris, still stooped, on the other side of the pond now, flung his stick away.

"For goodness' sake, don't fall in, but if you do—" Elinor forced herself to go on "—grab hold of these vines. You see? They're strong and growing from the edges. Pull yourself out by them." Actually, the vines seemed to be growing from underwater as well, and pulling at those might send Chris into the pond.

Chris grinned, sideways. "That's not deep. Not even deep as I am."

Elinor said nothing.

The rest of that morning she worked on her law article, then telephoned Miller Brothers.

"Well, the ground's a little low there, ma'am. Not to mention the old cesspool's nearby and it still gets the drain from the kitchen sink, even though the toilets've been put on the mains. We know that house. Pond'll get it too if you've got a washing machine in the kitchen."

Elinor hadn't. "You mean, draining it is hopeless."

"That's about the size of it."

Elinor tried to force her anger down. "Then I don't know why you agreed to do it."

"Because you seemed set on it, ma'am."

They hung up a few seconds later. What was she going to do about the bill when they presented it? She'd perhaps make them knock it down a bit. But she felt the situation was inconclusive. Elinor hated that.

While Chris was taking his nap, Elinor made a quick trip to Hartford, found a fish shop, and brought back a carp in a red plastic bucket which she had taken with her in the car. The fish flopped about in a vigorous way, and Elinor drove slowly, so the bucket wouldn't tip over. She went at once to the pond, and poured the fish in.

It was a fat, silvery carp. Its tail flicked the surface as it dove, then it rose and dove again, apparently happy in wider seas. Elinor smiled. The carp would surely eat some of the vines, the algae. She'd give it bread too. Carps could eat anything. Cliff had used to say there was nothing like carp to keep a pond or a lake clean. Above all, Elinor liked the idea that there was something *alive* in the pond besides vines. She started to walk back to the house, and found that a vine had encircled her left ankle. When she tried to kick her foot free, the vine tightened. She stooped and unwound it. That was one she hadn't whacked this morning. Or had it grown ten inches since this morning? Impossible. But now as she looked down at the pond and at its border, she couldn't see that she had accomplished much, even though she'd fished out quite a heap. The heap was a few feet away on the grass, in case she doubted it. Elinor blinked. She had the feeling that if she watched the pond closely, she'd be able to see the tentacles growing. She didn't like that idea.

Should she tell Chris about the carp? Elinor didn't want him trying to find it, poking into the water. On the other hand, if she didn't mention it, maybe he'd see it and have some crazy idea of catching it. Better to tell him, she decided.

So when Chris woke up, Elinor told him about the fish.

"You can toss some bread to him," Elinor said. "But don't try to catch him, because he likes the pond. He's going to help us keep it clean."

"You don't want ever to catch him?" Chris asked, with milk all over his upper lip.

He was thinking of Cliff, Elinor knew. Cliff had loved fishing. "We don't catch this one, Chris. He's our friend."

Elinor worked. She had set up her typewriter in a front corner room upstairs which had light from two windows. The article was coming along nicely. She had a lot of original material from newspaper clippings. The theme was alerting the public to free legal advice from small claims offices which most people didn't know existed. Lots of people let sums like $250 go by the board, because they thought it wasn't worth the trouble of a court fight. Elinor worked until 6:30. Dinner was simple tonight, macaroni and cheese with bacon, one of Chris's favorite dishes. With the dinner in the oven, Elinor took a quick bath and put on blue slacks and a fresh blouse. She paused to look at the photograph of Cliff on the dressing table—a photograph in a silver frame which had been a present from Cliff's parents one Christmas. It was an ordinary black and white enlargement, Cliff sitting on the bank of a stream, propped against a tree, an old straw hat tipped back on his head. That had been taken somewhere outside Evanston, on one of their summer trips to visit his parents. Cliff held a straw or a blade of grass lazily between his lips. His denim shirt was open at the neck. No one, looking at the hillbilly image, would imagine that Cliff had had to dress up in white tie a couple of times a month in Paris, Rome, London or Ankara. Cliff had been in the diplomatic service, assistant or deputy to American statesmen, gifted in languages, gifted in tact. He'd known how to use a pistol also, and once a month in New York he'd gone to a certain armory for practice. What had he done exactly? Elinor knew only sketchy anecdotes that Cliff had told her. He had done enough, however, to be paid a good salary, to be paid to keep silent, even to her. It had crossed her mind that his plane was wrecked to kill him, but she was sure that was absurd. Cliff hadn't been that important. His death had been an accident, not due to the weather but to a mechanical failure in the plane.

What would Cliff think of the pond? Elinor smiled wryly. Would he have it filled in with stones, turn it into a rock garden? Would he fill it in with earth? Would he pay no attention at all to the pond? Just call it "nature?"

Two days later, when Elinor was typing a final draft of her article, she stopped at noon and went out into the garden for some fresh air. She'd brought the kitchen scissors, and she cut two red roses and one white rose to put on the table at lunch. Then the pond caught her eye, a blaze of chartreuse in the sunlight.

"Good Lord!" she whispered.

The vines! The weeds! They were all over the surface. And they were again climbing onto the land. Well, this was one thing she could and would see about: she'd find an exterminator. She didn't care what poison they put down in the pond, if they could clear it. And of course she'd rescue the carp first, keep him in a bucket till the pond was safe again.

An exterminator was something Jane Caldwell might know about.

Elinor telephoned Jane before she started lunch. "This *pond,*" Elinor began and stopped, because she had so much to say about it. "I had it drained a few days ago, and now it's filled up again . . . No, that's not really the problem. I've given up the draining, it's the unbelievable vines. The way they grow! I wonder if you know a weed-killing company? I think it'll take professional—I mean, I don't think I can just toss some liquid poison in and get anywhere. You'll have to see this pond to believe it. It's like a jungle!"

"I know just the right people," Jane said. "They're called 'Weed-Killer,' so it's easy to remember. You've got a phone book there?"

Elinor had. Jane said Weed-Killer was very obliging and wouldn't make her wait a week before they turned up.

"How about you and Chris coming over for tea this afternoon?" Jane asked. "I just made a coconut cake."

"Love to. Thank you." Elinor felt cheered.

She made lunch for herself and Chris, and told him they were invited to tea at the house of their neighbor Jane, and that he'd meet a boy called Bill. After lunch, Elinor looked up Weed-Killer in the telephone book and rang them.

"It's a lot of weeds in a pond," Elinor said. "Can you deal with that?"

The man assured her they were experts at weeds in ponds, and promised to come the following morning. Elinor wanted to work for an hour or so until it was time to go to Jane's, but she felt compelled to catch the carp now, or to try to. If she failed, she'd tell the men about it tomorrow, and probably they'd have a net on a long handle and could catch it. Elinor took her vegetable sieve which had a handle some ten inches long, and also some pieces of bread.

Not seeing the carp, Elinor tossed the bread onto the surface. Some pieces floated, others sank and were trapped among the vines. Elinor circled the pond, her sieve ready. She had half filled the plastic bucket and it sat on the bank.

Suddenly she saw the fish. It was horizontal and motionless, a couple of inches under the surface. It was dead, she realized, and kept from the surface only by the vines that held it under. Dead from what? The water didn't look dirty, in fact was rather clear. What could kill a carp? Cliff had always said—

Elinor's eyes were full of tears. Tears for the carp? Nonsense. Tears of frustration, maybe. She stooped and tried to reach the carp with the sieve. The sieve was a foot short, and she wasn't going to muddy her tennis shoes by wading in. Not now. Best to work a bit this afternoon, and let the workmen lift it out tomorrow.

"What're you doing, Mommy?" Chris came trotting towards her.

"Nothing. I'm going to work a little now. I thought you were watching TV."

"It's no good. Where's the fish?"

Elinor took his wrist, swung him around. "The fish is fine. Now come back and we'll try the TV again." Elinor tried to think of something else that might amuse him. It wasn't one of his napping days, obviously. "Tell you what, Chris, you choose one of your toys to take to Bill. Make him a present. All right?"

"One of *my* toys?"

Elinor smiled. Chris was generous by nature and she meant to nurture this trait. "Yes, one of yours. Even one you like—like your paratrooper. Or one of your books. You choose it. Bill's going to be your friend, and you want to start out right, don't you?"

"Yes." And Chris seemed to be pondering already, going over his store of goodies in his room upstairs.

Elinor locked the back door with its bolt, which was on a level with her eyes. She didn't want Chris going into the garden, maybe seeing the carp. "I'll be in my room, and I'll see you at four. You might put on a clean pair of jeans at four—if you remember to."

Elinor worked, and quite well. It was pleasant to have a tea date to look forward to. Soon, she thought, she'd ask Jane and her husband for drinks. She didn't want people to think she was a melancholy widow. It had been three months since Cliff's death. Elinor thought she'd got over the worst of her grief in those first two weeks, the weeks of shock. Had she really? For the past six weeks she'd been able to work. That was something. Cliff's insurance plus his pension made her financially comfortable, but she needed to work to be happy.

When she glanced at her watch, it was ten to four. "Chrissy!" Elinor called to her half-open door. "Changed your jeans?"

She pushed open Chris's door across the hall. He was not in his room, and there were more toys and books on the floor than usual, indicating that Chris had been trying to select something to give Bill. Elinor went downstairs where the TV was still murmuring, but Chris wasn't in the living room. Nor was he in the kitchen. She saw that the back door was still bolted. Chris wasn't on the front lawn either. Of course he could have gone to the garden via the front door. Elinor unbolted the kitchen door and went out.

"Chris?" She glanced everywhere, then focused on the pond. She had seen a light-colored patch in its center. *"Chris!"* She ran.

He was face down, feet out of sight, blond head nearly submerged. Elinor plunged in, up to her knees, her thighs, seized Chris's legs and pulled him out, slipped, sat down in the water and got soaked as high as her breasts. She struggled to her feet, holding Chris by the waist. Shouldn't she try to let the water run out of his mouth? Elinor was panting.

She turned Chris onto his stomach, gently lifted his small body by the waist, hoping water would run from his nose and mouth, but she was too frantic to look. He was limp, soft in a way that frightened her. She pressed his rib cage, released it, raised him a little again. One had to do artificial respiration methodically, counting, she remembered. She did this. *Fifteen . . . sixteen . . .* Someone should be telephoning for a doctor. She couldn't do two things at once.

"Help!" she yelled. "Help me, *please!*" Could the people next door hear? The house was twenty yards away, and was anybody home?

She turned Chris over and pressed her mouth to his cool lips. She blew in, then released his ribs, trying to catch a gasp from him, a cough that would mean life again. He remained limp. She turned him on his stomach and resumed the artificial respiration. It was now or never, she knew. Senseless to waste time carrying him into the house for warmth. He could've been lying in the pond for an hour—in which case, she knew it was hopeless.

Elinor picked her son up and carried him towards the house. She went into the kitchen. There was a sagging sofa against the wall, and she put him there.

Then she telephoned Jane Caldwell, whose number was on the card by the telephone where Elinor had left it days ago. Since

Elinor didn't know a doctor in the vicinity, it made as much sense to call Jane as to search for a doctor's name.

"Hello, *Jane!*" Elinor said, her voice rising wildly. "I think Chris's drowned!—Yes! *Yes!* Can you get a doctor? Right away?" Suddenly the line was dead. Elinor hung up and went at once to Chris, started the rib-pressing again, Chris prone on the sofa with his face turned to one side. The activity soothed her a little.

The doorbell rang, and at the same time Elinor heard the latch of the door being opened. Then Jane called:

"Elinor?"

"In the kitchen!"

The doctor had dark hair and spectacles. He lifted Chris a little, felt for a pulse. "How long—how long was he . . ."

"I don't know. I was working upstairs. It was the pond in the garden."

The rest was confused to Elinor. She barely realized when the needle went into her own arm, though this was the most definite sensation she had for several minutes. Jane made tea. Elinor had a cup in front of her. When she looked at the sofa, Chris was not there.

"Where is he?" Elinor asked.

Jane gripped Elinor's hand. She sat opposite Elinor. "The doctor took Chris to the hospital. Chris is in good hands, you can be sure of that. This doctor delivered Bill. He's our doctor."

But from Jane's tone, Elinor knew it was all useless, and that Jane knew this too. Elinor's eyes drifted from Jane's face. She noticed a book lying on the cane bottom of the chair beside her. Chris had chosen his dotted numbers book to give to Bill, a book that Chris rather liked. He wasn't half through doing the drawings. Chris could count and he was doing quite well at reading too. *I wasn't doing so well at his age, I think,* Cliff had said not long ago.

Elinor began to weep.

"That's good. That's good for you," Jane said. "I'll stay here with you. Pretty soon we'll hear from the hospital. Maybe you want to lie down, Elinor?—I've got to make a phone call."

The sedative was taking effect. Elinor sat in a daze on the sofa, her head back against a pillow. The telephone rang and Jane took it. The hospital, Elinor supposed. She watched Jane's face, and knew. Elinor nodded her head, trying to spare Jane any words, but Jane said:

"They tried. I'm sure they did everything possible."

Jane said she would stay the night. She said she had arranged for Ed to pick up Bill at a house where she'd left him.

In the morning, Weed-Killer came, and Jane asked Elinor if she still wanted the job done.

"I thought you might've decided to move," Jane said.

Had she said that? Possibly. "But I do want it done."

The two Weed-Killer men got to work.

Jane made another telephone call, then told Elinor that a friend of hers called Millie was coming over at noon. When Millie arrived, Jane prepared a lunch of bacon and eggs for the three of them. Millie had blonde curly hair, blue eyes, and was very cheerful and sympathetic.

"I went by the doctor's," Millie said, "and his nurse gave me these pills for you. They're slightly sedative. He thinks they'd be good for you. Two a day, one before lunch, one before bedtime. So have one now."

They hadn't started lunch. Elinor took one. The workmen were just departing, and one man stuck his head in the door to say with a smile:

"All finished, ma'am. You shouldn't have any trouble any more."

During lunch, Elinor said, "I've got to see about the funeral."

"We'll help you. Don't think about it now," Jane said. "Try to eat a little."

Elinor ate a little, then slept on the sofa in the kitchen. She hadn't wanted to go up to her own bed. When she woke up, Millie was sitting in the wicker armchair, reading a book.

"Feeling better? Want some tea?"

"In a minute. You're awfully kind. I do thank you very much." She stood up. "I want to see the pond." She saw Millie's look of uneasiness. "They killed those vines today. I'd like to see what it looks like."

Millie went out with her. Elinor looked down at the pond and had the satisfaction of seeing that no vines lay on the surface, that some pieces of them had sunk like drowned things. Around the edge of the pond were stubs of vines already turning yellow and brownish, wilting. Before her eyes, one cropped tentacle curled sideways and down, as if in the throes of death. A primitive joy went through her, a sense of vengeance, of a wrong righted.

"It's a nasty pond," Elinor said to Millie. "It killed a carp. Can you imagine? I've never heard of a carp being—"

"I know. They must've been growing like blazes! But they're certainly finished now." Millie held out her hand for Elinor to take. "Don't think about it now."

Millie wanted to go back to the house. Elinor did not take her hand, but she came with Millie. "I'm feeling better. You mustn't give up all your time to me. It's very nice of you, since you don't even know me. But I've got to face my problems alone."

Millie made some polite reply.

Elinor really was feeling better. She'd have to go through the funeral next, Chris's funeral, but she sensed in herself a backbone, morale—whatever it was called. After the service for Chris— surely it would be simple—she'd invite her new neighbors, few as they might be, to her house for coffee or drinks or both. Food too. Elinor realized that her spirits had picked up because the pool was vanquished. She'd have it filled in with stones, with the agent's and also the owner's permission of course. Why should she retreat from the house? With stones showing just above the water, it would

look every bit as pretty, maybe prettier, and it wouldn't be dangerous for the next child who came to live here.

The service for Chris was at a small local church. The preacher
conducted a short, nondenominational ceremony. And afterwards,
around noon, Elinor did have eight or ten people to the house for
coffee, drinks and sandwiches. The strangers seemed to enjoy it.
Elinor even heard a few laughs among the group which gladdened
her heart. She hadn't as yet, rung up any of her New York friends
to tell them about Chris. Elinor realized that some people might
think that "strange" of her, but she felt that it would only sadden
her friends to tell them, that it would look like a plea for sympa-
thy. Better the strangers here who knew no grief, because they
didn't know her or Chris.

"You must be sure and get enough rest in the next days," said
a kindly, middle-aged woman whose husband stood solemnly
beside her. "We all think you've been awfully brave . . ."

Elinor gave Jane the dotted numbers book to take to Bill.

That night Elinor did sleep more than twelve hours and
awoke feeling better and calmer. Now she began to write the letters that she had to, to Cliff's parents, to her own mother and
father, and to three good friends in New York. She finished typing
her article. The next morning, she walked to the post office and
sent off her letters, and also her article to her agent in New York.
She spent the rest of the day sorting out Chris's clothing, his books
and toys, and she washed some of his clothes with a view to passing them on to Jane for Bill, providing Jane wouldn't think it
unlucky. Elinor didn't think Jane would think that. Jane telephoned in the afternoon to ask how she was.

"Is anyone coming to see you? From New York? A friend, I
mean?"

Elinor explained that she'd written to a few people, but she
wasn't expecting anyone. "I'm really feeling all right, Jane. You
mustn't worry."

By evening, Elinor had a neat carton of clothing ready to offer Jane, two more cartons of books and one of toys. If the clothes didn't fit Bill, then Jane might know a child they would fit. Elinor felt better for that. It was a lot better than collapsing in grief, she thought. Of course it was awful, a tragedy that didn't happen every day—losing a husband and a child in hardly more than three months. But Elinor was not going to succumb to it. She'd stay out the six months in the house here, come to terms with her loss, and emerge strong, someone able to give something to other people, not merely take.

She had two ideas for future articles. Which to do first? She decided to walk out into the garden, let her thoughts ramble. Maybe the radishes had come up? She'd have a look at the pond. Maybe it would be glassy smooth and clear. She must ask the Weed-Killer people when it would be safe to put in another carp—or two carps.

When she looked at the pond, she gave a short gasp. The vines had come *back*. They looked stronger than ever—not really longer, but more dense. Even as she watched, one tentacle, then a second actually moved, curved towards the land and seemed to grow an inch. That hadn't been due to the wind. The vines were growing visibly. Another green shoot poked its head above the water's surface. Elinor watched, fascinated, as if she beheld animate things, like snakes. Every inch or so along the vines a small green leaf sprouted, and Elinor was sure she could see some of these unfurling. The water looked clean, but she knew that was deceptive. The water was somehow poisonous. It had killed a carp. It had killed Chris. And she could still detect, she thought, the rather acid smell of the stuff the Weed-Killer men had put in.

There must be such a thing as digging the roots out, Elinor thought, even if Weed-Killer's stuff had failed. Elinor got the fork from the toolshed, and she took the clippers also. She thought of getting her rubber boots from the house, but was too eager to start to bother with them. She began by hacking all round the edge with the clippers. Some fresh vine ends cruised over the pond and jammed themselves amid other growing vines. The stems now seemed tough as plastic clotheslines, as if the herbicide had forti-fied them. Some had put down roots in the grass quite a distance from the pond. Elinor dropped the clippers and seized the fork. She had to dig deep to get at the roots, and when she finally pulled with her hands, the stems broke, leaving some roots still in the soil. Her right foot slipped, she went down on her left knee and strug-gled up again, both legs wet now. She was not going to be defeated.

As she sank the fork in, she saw Cliff's handsome, subtly smil-ing eyes in the photograph in the bedroom, Cliff with the blade of grass or hay between his lips, and he seemed to be nodding ever so slightly, approving. Her arms began to ache, her hands grew tired. She lost her right shoe in dragging her foot out of the water yet again, and she didn't bother trying to recover it. Then she slipped again, and sat down, water up to her waist now. Tired, angry, she still worked with the fork, trying to prize roots loose, and the water churned with a muddy fury. She might even be doing the damned roots good, she thought. Aerating them or something. Were they invincible? Why should they be? The sun poured down, overheating her, bringing nourishment to the green, Elinor knew.

Nature knows. That was Cliff's voice in her ears. Cliff sounded happy and at ease.

Elinor was half blinded by tears. Or was it sweat? *Chun-nk* went her fork. In a moment, when her arms gave out, she'd cross to the other side of the pond and attack that. She'd got some out. She'd make Weed-Killer come again, maybe pour kerosene on the pond and light it.

She got up on cramped legs and stumbled around to the other side. The sun warmed her shoulders though her feet were cold. In those few seconds that she walked, her thoughts and her attitude changed, though she was not at once aware of this. It was neither victory nor defeat that she felt. She sank the fork in again, again slipped and recovered. Again roots slid between the tines of the fork, and were not removed. A tentacle thicker than most moved towards her and circled her right ankle. She kicked, and the vine tightened, and she fell forward.

She went face down into the water, but the water seemed soft. She struggled a little, turned to breathe, and a vine tickled her neck. She saw Cliff nodding again, smiling his kindly, knowing, almost imperceptible smile. It was nature. It was Cliff. It was Chris. A vine crept around her arm—loose or attached to the earth she neither knew nor cared. She breathed in, and much of what she took in was water. *All things come from water,* Cliff had said once. Little Chris smiled at her with both corners of his mouth upturned. She saw him stooped by the pond, reaching for the dead carp which floated out of range of his twig. Then Chris lifted his face again and smiled.

Something You
Have to Live With

"Don't forget to lock all the doors," Stan said. "Someone might think because the car's gone, nobody's home."

"All the doors? You mean two. You haven't asked me anything—aesthetic, such as how the place looks now."

Stan laughed. "I suppose the pictures are all hung and the books are in the shelves."

"Well, not quite, but your shirts and sweaters—and the kitchen. It looks—I'm happy, Stan. So is Cassie. She's walking around the place purring. See you tomorrow morning then. Around eleven, you said?"

"Around eleven. I'll bring stuff for lunch, don't worry."

"Love to your mom. I'm glad she's better."

"Thanks, darling." Stan hung up.

Cassie, their ginger and white cat aged four, sat looking at Ginnie as if she had never seen a telephone before. Purring again. Dazed by all the space, Ginnie thought. Cassie began kneading the rug in an ecstasy of contentment, and Ginnie laughed.

Ginnie and Stan Brixton had bought a house in Connecticut after six years of New York apartments. Their furniture had been here for a week while they wound things up in New York, and yesterday had been the final move of smaller things like silverware, some dishes, a few pictures, suitcases, kitchen items and the cat. Stan had taken their son Freddie this morning to spend the night in New Hope, Pennsylvania, where Stan's mother lived. His mother had had a second heart attack and was recuperating at home. "Every time I see her, I think it may be the last. You don't mind if I go, do you, Ginnie? It'll keep Freddie out of the way while you're fiddling around." Ginnie hadn't minded.

Fiddling around was Stan's term for organizing and even cleaning. Ginnie thought she had done a good job since Stan and Freddie had taken off this morning. The lovely French blue and white vase which reminded Ginnie of Monet's paintings stood on the living room bookcase now, even bearing red roses from the garden. Ginnie had made headway in the kitchen, installing things the way she wanted them, the way they would remain. Cassie had her litter pan ("What a euphemism, litter ought to mean a bed," Stan said) in the downstairs john corner. They now had an upstairs bathroom also. The house was on a hill with no other houses around it for nearly a mile, not that they owned all the land around, but the land around was farmland. When she and Stan had seen the place in June, sheep and goats had been grazing not far away. They had both fallen in love with the house.

Stanley Brixton was a novelist and fiction critic, and Ginnie wrote articles and was now half through her second novel. Her first had been published but had had only modest success. You couldn't expect a smash hit with a first novel, Stan said, unless the publicity was extraordinary. Water under the bridge. Ginnie was more interested in her novel-in-progress. They had a mortgage on the house, and with her and Stan's freelance work they thought they could be independent of New York, at least independent of nine-to-five jobs. Stan had already published three books, adventure stories with a political slant. He was thirty-two and for three years had been overseas correspondent for a newspaper syndicate.

Ginnie picked up a piece of heavy twine from the living room rug, and realized that her back hurt a little from the day's exertions. She had thought of switching on the TV, but the news was just over, she saw from her watch, and it might be better to go straight to bed and get up earlyish in the morning.

"Cassie?"

Cassie replied with a courteous, sustained, "M-wah-h?"

"Hungry?" Cassie knew the word. "No, you've had enough. Do you know you're getting middle-aged spread? Come on. Going up to bed with me?" Ginnie went to the front door, which was already locked by its automatic lock, but she put the chain on also. Yawning, she turned out the downstairs lights and climbed the stairs. Cassie followed her.

Ginnie had a quick bath, second of the day, pulled on a nightgown, brushed her teeth and got into bed. She at once realized she was too tired to pick up one of the English weeklies, political and Stan's favorites, which she had dropped by the bed to look at. She put out the lamp. *Home.* She and Stan had spent one night here last weekend during the big move. This was the first night she had been alone in the house, which still had no name. *Something like White Elephant maybe,* Stan had said. *You think of something.* Ginnie tried to think, an activity which made her instantly sleepier.

She was awakened by a crunching sound, like that of car tires on gravel. She raised up a little in bed. Had she heard it? Their driveway hadn't any gravel to speak of, just unpaved earth. But—

Wasn't that a *click?* From somewhere. Front, back? Or had it been a twig falling on the roof?

She had locked the doors, hadn't she?

Ginnie suddenly realized that she had not locked the back door. For another minute, as Ginnie listened, everything was silent. What a bore to go downstairs again! But she thought she had better do it, so she could honestly tell Stan that she had. Ginnie found the lamp switch and got out of bed.

By now she was thinking that any noise she had heard had been imaginary, something out of a dream. But Cassie followed her in a brisk, anxious way, Ginnie noticed.

The glow from the staircase light enabled Ginnie to find her way to the kitchen, where she switched on the strong ceiling light. She went at once to the back door and turned the Yale bolt. Then she listened. All was silent. The big kitchen looked exactly the same with its half modern, half old-fashioned furnishings—electric stove, big white wooden cupboard with drawers below, shelves above, double sink, a huge new fridge.

Ginnie went back upstairs, Cassie still following. Cassie was short for Cassandra, a name Stan had given her when she had been a kitten, because she had looked gloomy, unshakably pessimistic. Ginnie was drifting off to sleep again, when she heard a bump downstairs, as if someone had staggered slightly. She switched on the bedside lamp again, and a thrust of fear went through her

when she saw Cassie rigidly crouched on the bed with her eyes
fixed on the open bedroom door.

Now there was another bump from downstairs, and the
unmistakable rustle of a drawer being slid out, and it could be only
the dining room drawer where the silver was.

She had locked someone in with her!

Her first thought was to reach for the telephone and get the
police, but the telephone was downstairs in the living room.

Go down and face it and threaten him with something—or them, she
told herself. Maybe it was an adolescent kid, just a local kid who'd
be glad to get off unreported, if she scared him a little. Ginnie
jumped out of bed, put on Stan's bathrobe, a sturdy blue flannel
thing, and tied the belt firmly. She descended the stairs. By now
she heard more noises.

"Who's *there?*" she shouted boldly.

"Hum-hum. Just me, lady," said a rather deep voice.

The living room lights, the dining room lights were full on.

In the dining room Ginnie was confronted by a stocking-
hooded figure in what she thought of as motorcycle gear: black
trousers, black boots, black plastic jacket. The stocking had slits cut
in it for eyes. And the figure carried a dirty canvas bag like a railway mailbag, and plainly into this the silverware had already gone,
because the dining room drawer gaped, empty. He must have been
hiding in a corner of the dining room, Ginnie thought, when she
had come down to lock the back door. The hooded figure shoved
the drawer in carelessly, and it didn't quite close.

"Keep your mouth shut, and you won't get hurt. All right?"
The voice sounded like that of a man of at least twenty-five.

Ginnie didn't see any gun or knife. "Just what do you think
you're doing?"

"What does it look like I'm doing?" And the man got on with
his business. The two candlesticks from the dining room table went
into the bag. So did the silver table lighter.

Was there anyone else with him? Ginnie glanced towards the

kitchen, but didn't see anyone, and no sound came from there. "I'm going to call the police," she said, and started for the living room telephone.

"Phone's cut, lady. You better keep quiet, because no one can hear you around here, even if you scream."

Was that true? Unfortunately it was true. Ginnie for a few seconds concentrated on memorizing the man's appearance: about five feet eight, medium build, maybe a bit slender, broad hands— but since the hands were in blue rubber gloves, were they broad?—rather big feet. Blond or brunette she couldn't tell, because of the stocking mask. Robbers like this usually bound and gagged people. Ginnie wanted to avoid that, if she could.

"If you're looking for money, there's not much in the house just now," Ginnie said, "except what's in my handbag upstairs, about thirty dollars. Go ahead and take it."

"I'll get around to it," he said laughing, prowling the living room now. He took the letter-opener from the coffee table, then Freddie's photograph from the piano, because the photograph was in a silver frame.

Ginnie thought of banging him on the head with—with what? She saw nothing heavy enough, portable, except one of the dining room chairs. And if she failed to knock him out with the first swat? Was the telephone really cut? She moved towards the telephone in the corner.

"Don't go near the door. Stay in sight!"

"Ma-wow-wow-*wow*!" This from Cassie, a high-pitched wail that to Ginnie meant Cassie was on the brink of throwing up, but now the situation was different. Cassie looked ready to attack the man.

"Go back, Cassie, take it easy," Ginnie said.

"I don't like cats," the hooded man said over his shoulder.

There was not much else he could take from the living room, Ginnie thought. The pictures on the walls were too big. And what burglar was interested in pictures, at least pictures like these which were a few oils done by their painter friends, two or three water-colors—Was this really happening? Was a stranger picking up her mother's old sewing basket, looking inside, banging it down again? Taking the French vase, tossing the water and roses towards the fireplace? The vase went into the sack.

"What's upstairs?" The ugly head turned towards her. "Let's go upstairs."

"There's *nothing* upstairs!" Ginnie shrieked. She darted towards the telephone, knowing it would be cut, but wanting to see it with her own eyes—cut—though her hand was outstretched to use it. She saw the abruptly stopped wire on the floor, cut some four feet from the telephone.

The hood chuckled. "Told you."

A red flashlight stuck out of the back pocket of his trousers. He was going into the hall now, ready to take the stairs. The stair-case light was on, but he pulled the flashlight from his pocket.

"Nothing *up* there, I tell you!" Ginnie found herself following him like a ninnie, holding up the hem of Stan's dressing gown so she wouldn't trip on the stairs.

"Cosy little nook!" said the hood, entering the bedroom. "And what have we here? Anything of interest?"

The silver-backed brush and comb on the dresser were of interest, also the hand mirror, and these went into the bag, which was now dragging the floor.

"Aha! I like that thing!" He had spotted the heavy wooden box with brass corners which Stan used for cufflinks and hand-kerchiefs and a few white ties, but its size was apparently daunting the man in the hood, because he swayed in front of it and said, "Be back for that." He looked around for lighter objects, and in went Ginnie's black leather jewelry box, her Dunhill lighter from the bedside table. "Ought to be glad I'm not raping you. Haven't the time." The tone was jocular.

My God, Ginnie thought, you'd think Stan and I were rich! She had never considered herself and Stan rich, or thought that they had anything worth invading a house for. No doubt in New York they'd been lucky for six years—no robberies at all—because even a typewriter was valuable to a drug addict. No, they weren't rich, but he was taking all they had, all the *nice* things they'd tried over the years to accumulate. Ginnie watched him open her hand-bag, lift the dollar bills from her billfold. That was the least of it.

"If you think for one minute you're going to get away with this," Ginnie said. "In a small community like *this*? You haven't a prayer. If you don't leave those things here tonight, I'll report you so quick—"

"Oh, shut up, lady. Where's the other rooms here?"

Cassie snarled. She had followed them both up the stairs.

A black boot struck out sideways and caught the cat sharply in the ribs.

"Don't touch that cat!" Ginnie cried out.

Cassie sprang growling onto the man's boot top, at his knee.

Ginnie was astounded—and proud of Cassie—for a second.

"Pain in the ass!" said the hood, and with a gloved hand caught the cat by the loose skin on her back and flung her against a wall with a backhand swing. The cat dropped, panting, and the man stomped on her side and kicked her on the head.

"You *bastard*!" Ginnie screamed.

"So much for your stinking—yowlers!" said the beige hood, and kicked the cat once again. His voice had been husky with rage, and now he stalked with his flashlight into the hall, in quest of other rooms.

Dazed, stiff, Ginnie followed him.

The guest room had only a chest of drawers in it, empty, but the man slid out a couple of drawers anyway to have a look. Freddie's room had nothing but a bed and table. The hood wasted no time there.

From the hall, Ginnie looked into the bedroom at her cat. The cat twitched and was still. One foot had twitched. Ginnie stood rigid as a column of stone. She had just seen Cassie die, she realized.

"Back in a flash," said the hooded man, briskly descending the stairs with his sack which was now so heavy he had to carry it on one shoulder.

Ginnie moved at last, in jerks, like someone awakening from an anesthetic. Her body and mind seemed not to be connected. Her hand reached for the stair rail and missed it. She was no longer afraid at all, though she did not consciously realize this. She simply kept following the hooded figure, her enemy, and would have kept on, even if he had pointed a gun at her. By the time she reached the kitchen, he was out of sight. The kitchen door was open, and a cool breeze blew in. Ginnie continued across the kitchen, looked left into the driveway, and saw a flashlight's beam swing as the man heaved the bag into a car. She heard the hum of two male voices. So he had a pal waiting for him!

And here he came back.

With sudden swiftness, Ginnie picked up a kitchen stool which had a square formica top and chromium legs. As soon as the hooded figure stepped onto the threshold of the kitchen, Ginnie swung the stool and hit him full on the forehead with the edge of the stool's seat.

Momentum carried the man forward, but he stooped, staggering, and Ginnie cracked him again on the top of the head with all her strength. She held two legs of the stool in her hands. He fell with a great thump and clatter onto the linoleum floor. Another whack for good measure on the back of the stockinged head. She felt pleased and relieved to see blood coming through the beige material.

"Frankie?—You okay?—*Frankie!*"

The voice came from the car outside.

Poised now, not at all afraid, Ginnie stood braced for the next arrival. She held a leg of the stool in her right hand, and her left supported the seat. She awaited, barely two feet from the open door, the sound of boots in the driveway, another figure in the doorway.

Instead, she heard a car motor start, saw a glow of its lights through the door. The car was backing down the drive.

Finally Ginnie set the stool down. The house was silent again. The man on the floor was not moving. Was he dead?

I don't care. I simply don't give a damn, Ginnie said inside herself.

But she did care. What if he woke up? What if he needed a doctor, a hospital right away? And there was no telephone. The nearest house was nearly a mile away, the village a good mile. Ginnie would have to walk it with a flashlight. Of course if she encountered a car, a car might stop and ask what was the matter, and then she could tell someone to fetch a doctor or an ambulance. These thoughts went through Ginnie's head in seconds, and then she returned to the facts. The fact was, he *might* be dead. Killed by her.

So was Cassie dead. Ginnie turned towards the living room. Cassie's death was more real, more important than the body at her feet which only might be dead. Ginnie drew a glass of water for herself at the kitchen sink.

Everything was silent outside. Now Ginnie was calm enough to realize that the robber's chum had thought it best to make a getaway. He probably wasn't coming back, not even with reinforcements. After all, he had the loot in his car—silverware, her jewelry box, all the nice things.

Ginnie stared at the long black figure on her kitchen floor. He hadn't moved at all. The right hand lay under him, the left arm was outstretched, upward. The stockinged head was turned slightly towards her, one slit showing. She couldn't see what was going on behind that crazy slit.

"Are you *awake*?" Ginnie said, rather loudly.

She waited.

She knew she would have to face it. Best to feel the pulse in the wrist, she thought, and at once forced herself to do this. She pulled the rubber glove down a bit, and gripped a blondish-haired wrist which seemed to her of astonishing breadth, much wider than Stan's wrist, anyway. She couldn't feel any pulse. She altered the place where she had put her thumb, and tried again. There was no pulse.

So she had murdered someone. The fact did not sink in.

Two thoughts danced in her mind: she would have to remove Cassie, put a towel or something around her, and she was not going to be able to sleep or even remain in this house with a corpse lying on the kitchen floor.

Ginnie got a dishtowel, a folded clean one from a stack on a shelf, took a second one, went to the hall and climbed the stairs. Cassie was now bleeding. Rather, she had bled. The blood on the carpet looked dark. One of Cassie's eyes projected from the socket. Ginnie gathered her as gently as if she were still alive and only injured, gathered up some intestines which had been pushed out, and enfolded her in a towel, opened the second towel and put that around her too. Then she carried Cassie to the living room, hesitated, then laid the cat's body to one side of the fireplace on the floor. By accident, a red rose lay beside Cassie.

Tackle the blood now, she told herself. She got a plastic bowl from the kitchen, drew some cold water and took a sponge. Upstairs, she went to work on hands and knees, changing the water in the bathroom. The task was soothing, as she had known it would be.

Next job: clothes on and find the nearest telephone. Ginnie kept moving, barely aware of what she was doing, and suddenly she was standing in the kitchen in blue jeans, sneakers, sweater and jacket with her billfold in a pocket. Empty billfold, she remembered. She had her house keys in her left hand. For no good reason, she decided to leave the kitchen light on. The front door was still locked, she realized. She found she had the flashlight in a jacket pocket too, and supposed she had taken it from the front hall table when she came down the stairs.

She went out, locked the kitchen door from the outside with a key, and made her way to the road.

No moon at all. She walked with the aid of the flashlight

along the left side of the road towards the village, shone the torch
once on her watch and saw that it was twenty past one. By
starlight, by a bit of flashlight, she saw one house far to the left in
a field, quite dark and so far away, Ginnie thought she might do
better to keep on.

She kept on. Dark road. Trudging. Did *everybody* go to bed
early around here?

In the distance she saw two or three white streetlights, the
lights of the village. Surely there'd be a car before the village.

There wasn't a car. Ginnie was still trudging as she entered the
village proper, whose boundary was marked by a neat white sign
on either side of the road saying EAST KINDALE.

My God, Ginnie thought. *Is this true? Is this what I'm doing,
what I'm going to say?*

Not a light showed in any of the neat, mostly white houses.
There was not even a light at the Connecticut Yankee Inn, the
only functioning hostelry and bar in town, Stan had remarked
once. Nevertheless, Ginnie marched up the steps and knocked on
the door. Then with her flashlight, she saw a brass knocker on the
white door, and availed herself of that.

Rap-rap-rap!

Minutes passed. *Be patient,* Ginnie told herself. *You're overwrought.*
But she felt compelled to rap again.

"Who's there?" a man's voice called.

"A neighbor! There's been an accident!"

Ginnie fairly collapsed against the figure who opened the
door. It was a man in a plaid woolen bathrobe and pajamas. She
might have collapsed also against a woman or a child.

Then she was sitting on a straight chair in a sort of living
room. She had blurted out the story.

"We'll—we'll get the police right away, ma'am. Or an ambulance, as you say. But from what you say—" The man talking was
in his sixties, and sleepy.

His wife, more efficient looking, had joined him to listen. She wore a dressing gown and pink slippers. "Police, Jake. Man sounds dead from what the lady says. Even if he isn't, the police'll know what to do."

"Hello, Ethel! That you?" the man said into the telephone. "Listen, we need the police right away. You know the old Hardwick place? . . . Tell 'em to go there . . . No, *not* on fire. Can't explain now. But somebody'll be there to open the door in—in about five minutes."

The woman pushed a glass of something into Ginnie's hand. Ginnie realized that her teeth were chattering. She was cold, though it wasn't cold outside. It was early September, she remembered.

"They're going to want to speak with you." The man who had been in the plaid robe was now in trousers and a belted sports jacket. "You'll have to tell them the time it happened and all that."

Ginnie realized. She thanked the woman and went with the man to his car. It was an ordinary four-door, and Ginnie noticed a discarded Cracker Jack box on the floor of the passenger's seat as she got in.

A police car was in the drive. Someone was knocking on the back door, and Ginnie saw that she'd left the kitchen light on.

"Hya, Jake! What's up?" called a second policeman, getting out of the black car in the driveway.

"Lady had a house robbery," the man with Ginnie explained. "She thinks—Well, you've got the keys, haven't you, Mrs. Brixton?"

"Oh yes, yes." Ginnie fumbled for them. She was gasping again, and reminded herself that it was a time to keep calm, to answer questions accurately. She opened the kitchen door.

A policeman stooped beside the prone figure. "Dead," he said.

"The—Mrs. Brixton said she hit him with the kitchen stool. That one, ma'am?" The man called Jake pointed to the yellow formica stool.

"Yes. He was coming *back,* you see. You see—" Ginnie choked and gave up, for the moment.

Jake cleared his throat and said, "Mrs. Brixton and her husband just moved in. Husband isn't here tonight. She'd left the kitchen door unlocked and two—well, one fellow came in, this one. He went out with a bag of stuff he'd taken, put it in a waiting car, then came back to get more, and that's when Mrs. Brixton hit him."

"Um-*hum,*" said the policeman, still stooped on his heels. "Can't touch the body till the detective gets here. Can I use your phone, Mrs. Brixton?"

"They cut the phone," Jake said. "That's why she had to walk to my place."

The other policeman went out to telephone from his car. The policeman who remained put on water for coffee (or had he said tea?), and chatted with Jake about tourists, about someone they both knew who had just got married—as if they had known each other for years. Ginnie was sitting on one of the dining room chairs. The policeman asked where the instant coffee was, if she had any, and Ginnie got up to show him the coffee jar which she had put on a cabinet shelf beside the stove.

"Terrible introduction to a new house," the policeman remarked, holding his steaming cup. "But we all sure hope—" Suddenly his words seemed to dry up. His eyes flickered and looked away from Ginnie's face.

A couple of men in plainclothes arrived. Photographs were taken of the dead man. Ginnie went over the house with one of the men, who made notes of the items Ginnie said were stolen. No, she hadn't seen the color of the car, much less the license plate. The body on the floor was wrapped and carried out on a stretcher. Ginnie had only a glimpse of that, from which the detective even tried to shield her. Ginnie was in the dining room then, reckoning up the missing silver.

"I didn't mean to kill him!" Ginnie cried out suddenly, interrupting the detective. "Not *kill* him, honestly!"

STAN ARRIVED VERY early, about 8 A.M., with Freddie, and went to the Inn to fetch Ginnie. Ginnie had spent the night there, and someone had telephoned Stan at the number Ginnie had given.

"She's had a shock," Jake said to Stan.

Stan looked bewildered. But at least he had heard what happened, and Ginnie didn't have to go over it.

"All the nice things we had," Ginnie said. "And the cat—"

"The police might get our stuff back, Ginnie. If not, we'll buy more. We're all safe, at least." Stan set his firm jaw, but he smiled. He glanced at Freddie who stood in the doorway, looking a little pale from lack of sleep. "Come on. We're going home."

He took Ginnie's hand. His hand felt warm, and she realized her own hands were cold again.

They tried to keep the identity of the dead man from her, Ginnie knew, but on the second day she happened to see it printed—on a folded newspaper which lay on the counter in the grocery store. There was a photograph of him too, a blondish fellow with curly hair and a rather defiant expression. *Frank Collins, 24, of Hartford* . . .

Stan felt that they ought to go on living in the house, gradually buy the "nice things" again that Ginnie kept talking about. Stan said she ought to get back to work on her novel.

"I don't want any nice things any more. Not again." That was true, but that was only part of it. The worst was that she had killed someone, stopped a life. She couldn't fully realize it, therefore couldn't believe it somehow, or understand it.

"At least we could get another cat."

"Not yet," she said.

People said to her (like Mrs. Durham, Gladys, who lived a mile or so out of East Kindale on the opposite side from the Brixtons), "You mustn't reproach yourself. You did it in defense of your house. Don't you think a lot of us wish we had the courage, if someone comes barging in intending to rob you . . ."

"I wouldn't hesitate—to do what you did!" That was from perky Georgia Hamilton, a young married woman with black curly hair, active in local politics, who lived in East Kindale proper.

She came especially to call on Ginnie and to make acquaintance with her and Stan. "These hoodlums from miles away—Hartford!—they come to rob us, just because they think we still have some family silver and a few *nice* things . . ."

There was the phrase again, the *nice* things.

Stan came home one day with a pair of silver candlesticks for the dining room table. "Less than a hundred dollars, and we can afford them," Stan said.

To Ginnie they looked like bait for another robbery. They were pretty, yes. Georgian. Modern copy, but still beautiful. She could not take any aesthetic pleasure from them.

"Did you take a swat at your book this afternoon?" Stan asked cheerfully. He had been out of the house nearly three hours that afternoon. He had made sure the doors were locked, for Ginnie's sake, before he left. He had also bought a metal wheelbarrow for use in the garden, and it was still strapped to the roof of the car.

"No," Ginnie said. "But I suppose I'm making progress. I have to get back to a state of concentration, you know."

"Of course I know," Stan said. "I'm a writer too."

The police had never recovered the silverware, or Ginnie's leather box which had held her engagement ring (it had become too small and she hadn't got around to having it enlarged), and her grandmother's gold necklace and so forth. Stan told Ginnie they had checked all the known pals of the man who had invaded the house, but hadn't come up with anything. The police thought the dead man might have struck up acquaintance with his chum very recently, possibly the same night as the robbery.

"Darling," Stan said, "do you think we should *move* from this house? I'm willing—if it'd make you feel—less—"

Ginnie shook her head. It wasn't the house. She didn't any longer (after two months) even think of the corpse on the floor when she went into the kitchen. It was something inside her. "No," Ginnie said.

"Well—I think you ought to talk to a psychiatrist. Just one

visit even," Stan added, interrupting a protest from Ginnie. "It isn't enough for neighbors to say you did the natural thing. Maybe you need a professional to tell you." Stan chuckled. He was in tennis shoes and old clothes, and had had a good day at the typewriter.

Ginnie agreed, to please Stan.

The psychiatrist was in Hartford, a man recommended to Stan by a local medical doctor. Stan drove Ginnie there, and waited for her in the car. It was to be an hour's session, but Ginnie reappeared after about forty minutes.

"He gave me some pills to take," Ginnie said.

"Is *that* all?—But what did he say?"

"Oh." Ginnie shrugged. "The same as they all say, that— nobody blames me, the police didn't make a fuss, so what—" She shrugged again, glanced at Stan and saw the terrible disappoint- ment in his face as he looked from her into the distance through the windshield.

Ginnie knew he was thinking again about "guilt" and aban- doning it, abandoning the word again. She had said no, she didn't feel guilty, that wasn't the trouble, that would have been too sim- ple. She felt disturbed, she had said many times, and she couldn't do anything about it.

"You really ought to write a book about it, a novel," Stan said—this for at least the fourth time.

"And how can I, if I can't come to terms with it myself, if I can't even analyze it first?" This Ginnie said for at least the third time and possibly the fourth. It was as if she had an unsolvable mystery within her. "You can't write a book just stammering around on paper."

Stan then started the car.

The pills were mild sedatives combined with some kind of mild picker-uppers. They didn't make change in Ginnie.

Two more months passed. Ginnie resisted buying any "nice things," so they had nothing but the nice candlesticks. They ate with stainless steel. Freddie pulled out of his period of tension and suppressed excitement (he knew quite well what had happened in the kitchen), and in Ginnie's eyes became quite normal again, whatever normal was. Ginnie got back to work on the book she had started before moving to the house. She didn't ever dream about the murder, or manslaughter, in fact she often thought it might be better if she did dream about it.

But among people—and it was a surprisingly friendly region, they had all the social life they could wish—she felt compelled to say sometimes, when there was a lull in the conversation:

"Did you know, by the way, I once killed a man?"

Everyone would look at her, except of course those who had heard her say this before, maybe three times before.

Stan would grow tense and blank-minded, having failed once more to spring in in time before Ginnie got launched. He was jittery at social gatherings, trying like a fencer to dart in with something, anything to say, before Ginnie made her big thrust. *It's just something they, he and Ginnie, had to live with,* Stan told himself.

And it probably would go on and on, even maybe when Freddie was twelve and even twenty. It had, in fact, half-ruined their marriage. But it was emphatically not worth divorcing for. He still loved Ginnie. She was still Ginnie after all. She was just somehow different. Even Ginnie had said that about herself.

"It's something I just have to live with," Stan murmured to himself.

"What?" It was Georgia Hamilton on his left, asking him what he had said. "Oh, I know, I know." She smiled understandingly. "But maybe it does her good."

Ginnie was in the middle of her story. At least she always made it short, and even managed to laugh in a couple of places.

Slowly, Slowly
in the Wind

Edward (Skip) Skipperton spent most of his life in a thunderous rage. It was his nature. He had been full of temper as a boy, and as a man impatient with people's slowness or stupidity or inefficiency. Now Skipperton was fifty-two. His wife had left him two years ago, unable to stand his tantrums any longer. She had met a most tranquil university professor from Boston, had divorced Skipperton on the grounds of incompatibility, and married the professor. Skipperton had been determined to get custody of their daughter, Margaret, then fifteen, and with clever lawyers and on the grounds that his wife had deserted him for another man, Skipperton had succeeded. A few months after the divorce, Skipperton had a heart attack, a real stroke with hemi-paralysis from which he miraculously recovered in six months, but his doctors gave him warning.

"Skip, it's life or death. You quit smoking and drinking and right now, or you're a dead man before your next birthday." That was from his heart specialist.

"You owe it to Margaret," said his GP. "You ought to retire, Skip. You've plenty of money. You're in the wrong profession for your nature—granted you've made a success of it. But what's left of your life is more important, isn't it? Why not become a gentleman farmer, something like that?"

Skipperton was a management adviser. Behind the scenes of big business, Skipperton was well known. He worked freelance. Companies on the brink sent for him to reorganize, reform, throw out—anything Skip advised went. "I go in and kick the ass off 'em!" was the inelegant way Skip described his work when he was interviewed, which was not often, because he preferred a ghostly role.

Skipperton bought Coldstream Heights in Maine, a seven-acre farm with a modernized farmhouse, and hired a local man called Andy Humbert to live and work on the place. Skipperton also bought some of the machinery the former owner had to sell, but not all of it, because he didn't want to turn himself into a full-

time farmer. The doctors had recommended a little exercise and
no strain of any kind. They had known that Skip wouldn't and
couldn't at once cut all his connections with the businesses he had
helped in the past. He might have to make an occasional trip to
Chicago or Dallas, but he was officially retired.

Margaret was transferred from her private school in New York
to a Swiss boarding school. Skipperton knew and liked Switzerland, and had bank accounts there.

Skipperton did stop drinking and smoking. His doctors were
amazed at his willpower—and yet it was just like Skip to stop
overnight, like a soldier. Now Skip chewed his pipes, and went
through a stem in a week. He went through two lower teeth, but
got them capped in steel in Bangor. Skipperton and Andy kept a
couple of goats to crop the grass, and one sow who was pregnant
when Skip bought her, and who now had twelve piglets. Margaret
wrote filial letters saying she liked Switzerland and that her French
was improving no end. Skipperton now wore flannel shirts with
no tie, low boots that laced, and woodsmen's jackets. His appetite
had improved, and he had to admit he felt better.

The only thorn in his side—and Skipperton had to have one
to feel normal—was the man who owned some adjacent land, one
Peter Frosby, who wouldn't sell a stretch Skipperton offered to buy
at three times the normal price. This land sloped down to a little
river called the Coldstream, which in fact separated part of Skipperton's property from Frosby's to the north, and Skipperton
didn't mind that. He was interested in the part of the river nearest
him and in view from Coldstream Heights. Skipperton wanted to
be able to fish a little, to be able to say he owned that part of the
landscape and had riparian rights. But old Frosby didn't want
anybody fishing in his stream, Skipperton had been told by the
agents, even though Frosby's house was upstream and out of sight
of Skipperton's.

The week after Peter Frosby's rejection, Skipperton invited
Frosby to his house. "Just to get acquainted—as neighbors," Skip-

perton said on the telephone to Frosby. By now Skipperton had been living at Coldstream Heights for four months.

Skipperton had his best whiskey and brandy, cigars and cigarettes—all the things he couldn't enjoy himself—on hand when Frosby arrived in a dusty but new Cadillac, driven by a young man whom Frosby introduced as his son, Peter.

"The Frosbys don't sell their land," Frosby told Skipperton. "We've had the same land for nearly three hundred years, and the river's always been ours." Frosby, a skinny but strong-looking man with cold gray eyes puffed his cigar daintily and after ten minutes hadn't finished his first whiskey. "Can't see why you want it."

"A little fishing," Skipperton said, putting on a pleasant smile. "It's in view of my house. Just to be able to wade, maybe, in the summer." Skipperton looked at Peter Junior, who sat with folded arms beside and behind his father. Skipperton was backed only by shambly Andy, a good enough handyman, but not part of his dynasty. Skipperton would have given anything (except his life) to have been holding a straight whiskey in one hand and a good cigar in the other. "Well, I'm sorry," Skipperton said finally. "But I think you'll agree the price I offer isn't bad—twenty thousand cash for about two hundred yards of riparian rights. Doubt if you'll get it again—in your lifetime."

"Not interested in my lifetime," Frosby said with a faint smile. "I've got a son here."

The son was a handsome boy with dark hair and sturdy shoulders, taller than his father. His arms were still folded across his chest, as if to illustrate his father's negative attitude. He had unbent only briefly to light a cigarette which he had soon put out. Still, Peter Junior smiled as he and his father were leaving, and said:

"Nice job you've done with the Heights, Mr. Skipperton. Looks better than it did before."

"Thank you," Skip said, pleased. He had installed good leather-upholstered furniture, heavy floor-length curtains, and brass firedogs and tongs for the fireplace.

"Nice old-fashioned touches," Frosby commented in what seemed to Skipperton a balance between compliment and sneer. "We haven't seen a scarecrow around here in maybe—almost before my time, I think."

"I like old-fashioned things—like fishing," Skipperton said. "I'm trying to grow corn out there. Somebody told me the land was all right for corn. That's where a scarecrow belongs, isn't it? In a cornfield?" He put on as friendly a manner as he could, but his blood was boiling. A mule-stubborn Maine man, Frosby, sitting on several hundred acres that his more forceful ancestors had acquired for him.

Frosby Junior was peering at a photograph of Maggie, which stood in a silver frame on the hall table. She had been only thirteen or fourteen when the picture had been taken, but her slender face framed in long dark hair showed the clean-cut nose and brows, the subtle smile that would turn her into a beauty one day. Maggie was nearly eighteen now, and Skip's expectations were being confirmed.

"Pretty girl," said Frosby Junior, turning towards Skipperton, then glancing at his father, because they were all lingering in the hall.

Skipperton said nothing. The meeting had been a failure. Skipperton wasn't used to failures. He looked into Frosby's greenish-gray eyes and said, "I've one more idea. Suppose we make an arrangement that I rent the land for the duration of my life, and then it goes to you—or your son. I'll give you five thousand a year. Want to think it over?"

Frosby put on another frosty smile. "I think not, Mr. Skipperton. Thanks anyway."

"You might talk to your lawyer about it. No rush on my part."

Frosby now chuckled. "We know as much about law as the lawyers here. We know our boundaries anyway. Nice to meet you, Mr. Skipperton. Thank you for the whiskey and—good-bye."

No one shook hands. The Cadillac moved off.

"Damn the bastard," Skipperton muttered to Andy, but he

smiled. Life was a game, after all. You won sometimes, you lost sometimes.

It was early May. The corn was in, and Skipperton had spotted three or four strong green shoots coming through the beige, well-turned earth. That pleased him, made him think of American Indians, the ancient Mayans. Corn! And he had a classic scarecrow that he and Andy had knocked together a couple of weeks ago. They had dressed the crossbars in an old jacket, and the two sticks—nailed to the upright—in brown trousers. Skip had found the old clothes in the attic. A straw hat jammed onto the top and secured with a nail completed the picture.

Skip went off to San Francisco for a five-day operation on an aeronautics firm which was crippled by a lawsuit, scared to death by unions and contract pull-outs. Skip left them with more redundancies, three vice-presidents fired, but he left them in better shape, and collected fifty thousand for his work.

By way of celebrating his achievement and the oncoming summer that would bring Maggie, Skip shot one of Frosby's hunting dogs which had swum the stream onto his property to retrieve a bird. Skipperton had been waiting patiently at his bedroom window upstairs, knowing a shoot was on from the sound of guns. Skip had his binoculars and a rifle of goodly range. Let Frosby complain! Trespassing was trespassing.

Skip was almost pleased when Frosby took him to court over the dog. Andy had buried the dog, on Skipperton's orders, but Skipperton readily admitted the shooting. And the judge ruled in Skipperton's favor.

Frosby went pale with anger. "It may be the law but it's not human. It's not fair."

And a lot of good it did Frosby to say that!

Skipperton's corn grew high as the scarecrow's hips, and higher. Skip spent a lot of time up in his bedroom, binoculars and loaded rifle at hand, in case anything else belonging to Frosby showed itself on his land.

"Don't hit me," Andy said with an uneasy laugh. "You're shooting on the edge of the cornfield there, and now and then I weed it, y'know."

"You think there's something wrong with my eyesight?" Skip replied.

A few days later Skip proved there was nothing wrong with his eyesight, when he plugged a gray cat stalking a bird or a mouse in the high grass this side of the stream. Skip did it with one shot. He wasn't even sure the cat belonged to Frosby.

This shot produced a call in person from Frosby Junior the following day.

"It's just to ask a question, Mr. Skipperton. My father and I heard a shot yesterday, and last night one of our cats didn't come back at night to eat, and not this morning either. Do you know anything about that?" Frosby Junior had declined to take a seat.

"I shot the cat. It was on my property," Skipperton said calmly.

"But the cat—What harm was the cat doing?" The young man looked steadily at Skipperton.

"The law is the law. Property is property."

Frosby Junior shook his head. "You're a hard man, Mr. Skipperton." Then he departed.

Peter Frosby served a summons again, and the same judge ruled that in accordance with old English law and also American law, a cat was a rover by nature, not subject to constraint as was a dog. He gave Skipperton the maximum fine of one hundred dollars, and a warning not to use his rifle so freely in future.

That annoyed Skipperton, though of course he could and did laugh at the smallness of the fine. If he could think of something else annoying, something really *telling,* old Frosby might relent and at least lease some of the stream, Skip thought.

But he forgot the feud when Margaret came. Skip fetched her at the airport in New York, and they drove up to Maine. She looked taller to Skip, more filled out, and there were roses in her cheeks. She was a beauty, all right!

"Got a surprise for you at home," Skip said.

"Um-m—a horse maybe? I told you I learned to jump this year, didn't I?"

Had she? Skip said, "Yes. Not a horse, no."

Skip's surprise was a red Toyota convertible. He had remembered at least that Maggie's school had taught her to drive. She was thrilled, and flung her arms around Skip's neck.

"You're a darling, Daddy! And you know, you're looking *very* fell!"

Margaret had been to Coldstream Heights for two weeks at Easter, but now the place looked more cared for. She and Skip had arrived around midnight, but Andy was still up watching television in his own little house on the grounds, and Maggie insisted on going over to greet him. Skip was gratified to see Andy's eyes widen at the sight of her.

Skip and Maggie tried the new car out the next day. They drove to a town some twenty miles away and had lunch. That afternoon, back at the house, Maggie asked if her father had a fishing rod, just a simple one, so she could try the stream. Skip of course had all kinds of rods, but he had to tell her she couldn't, and he explained why, and explained that he had even tried to rent part of the stream.

"Frosby's a real s.o.b.," Skip said. "Won't give an inch."

"Well, never mind, Daddy. There's lots else to do."

Maggie was the kind of girl who enjoyed taking walks, reading or fussing around in the house rearranging little things so that they looked prettier. She did these things while Skip was on the telephone sometimes for an hour or so with Dallas or Detroit.

Skipperton was a bit surprised one day when Maggie arrived in her Toyota around 7 P.M. with a catch of three trout on a string. She was barefoot, and the cuffs of her blue dungarees were damp. "Where'd you get those?" Skip asked, his first thought being that she'd taken one of his rods and fished the stream against his instructions.

"I met the boy who lives there," Maggie said. "We were both buying gas, and he introduced himself—said he'd seen my photograph in your house. Then we had a coffee in the diner there by the gas station—"

"The Frosby boy?"

"Yes. He's awfully nice, Daddy. Maybe it's only the father who's not nice. Anyway Pete said, 'Come on and fish with me this afternoon,' so I did. He said his father stocks the river farther up."

"I don't—Frankly, Maggie, I *don't* want you associating with the Frosbys!"

"There's only two." Maggie was puzzled. "I barely met his father. They've got quite a nice house, Daddy."

"I've had unpleasant dealings with old Frosby, I told you, Maggie. It just isn't fitting if you get chummy with the son. Do me this one favor this summer, Maggie doll." That was his name for her in the moments he wanted to feel close to her, wanted her to feel close to him.

The very next day, Maggie was gone from the house for nearly three hours, and Skip noticed it. She had said she wanted to go to the village to buy sneakers, and she was wearing the sneakers when she came home, but Skip wondered why it had taken her three hours to make a five-mile trip. With enormous effort, Skip refrained from asking a question. Then Saturday morning, Maggie said there was a dance in Keensport, and she was going.

"And I have a suspicion who you're going with," Skip said, his heart beginning to thump with adrenaline.

"I'm going alone, I swear it, Daddy. Girls don't have to be escorted any more. I could go in blue jeans, but I'm not. I've got some white slacks."

Skipperton realized that he could hardly forbid her to go to a dance. But he damn well knew the Frosby boy would be there, and would probably meet Maggie at the entrance. "I'll be glad when you go back to Switzerland."

Skip knew what was going to happen. He could see it a mile

away. His daughter was "infatuated," and he could only hope that she got over it, that nothing happened before she had to go back to school (another whole month), because he didn't want to keep her prisoner in the house. He didn't want to look absurd in his own eyes, even in simpleminded Andy's eyes, by laying down the law to her.

Maggie got home evidently very late that night, and so quietly Skip hadn't wakened, though he had stayed up till 2 A.M. and meant to listen for her. At breakfast, Maggie looked fresh and radiant, rather to Skip's surprise.

"I suppose the Frosby boy was at the dance last night?"

Maggie, diving into bacon and eggs, said, "I don't know what you've got against him, Daddy—just because his father didn't want to sell land that's been in their family for ages!"

"I don't want you to fall in love with a country bumpkin! I've sent you to a good school. You've got background—or at least I intend to give you some!"

"Did you know Pete had three years at Harvard—and he's taking a correspondence course in electronic engineering?"

"Oh! I suppose he's learning computer programming? Easier than shorthand!"

Maggie stood up. "I'll be eighteen in another month, Daddy. I don't want to be told whom I can see and can't see."

Skip got up too and roared at her. *"They're not my kind of people or yours!"*

Maggie left the room.

In the next days, Skipperton fumed and went through two or three pipe stems. Andy noticed his unease, Skipperton knew, but Andy made no comment. Andy spent his nonworking hours alone, watching drivel on his television. Skip was rehearsing a speech to Maggie as he paced his land, glancing at the sow and piglets, at Andy's neat kitchen-garden, not seeing anything. Skip was groping for a lever, the kind of weapon he had always been able to find in business affairs that would force things his way. He couldn't send Maggie back to Switzerland, even though her school stayed open in summer for girls whose home was too far away to go back to. If he threatened not to send her back to school, he was afraid Maggie wouldn't mind. Skipperton maintained an apartment in New York, and had two servants who slept in, but he knew Maggie wouldn't agree to go there, and Skip didn't want to go to New York either. He was too interested in the immediate scene in which he sensed a battle coming.

Skipperton had arrived at nothing by the following Saturday, a week after the Keensport dance, and he was exhausted. That Saturday evening, Maggie said she was going to a party at the house of someone called Wilmers, whom she had met at the dance. Skip asked her for the address, and Maggie scribbled it on the hall telephone pad. Skip had reason to have asked for it, because by Sunday morning Maggie hadn't come home. Skip was up at seven, nervous as a cat and in a rage still at 9 A.M., which he thought a polite enough hour to telephone on Sunday morning, though it had cost him much to wait that long.

An adolescent boy's voice said that Maggie had been there, yes, but she had left pretty early.

"Was she alone?"

"No, she was with Pete Frosby."

"That's all I wanted to know," said Skip, feeling the blood rush to his face as if he were hemorrhaging. "*Oh!* Wait! Do you know where they went?"

"Sure don't."

"My daughter went in her car?"

"No, Pete's. Maggie's car's still here."

Skip thanked the boy and put the phone down shakily, but he was shaking only from energy that was surging through every nerve and muscle. He picked up the telephone and dialed the Frosby home.

Old Frosby answered.

Skipperton identified himself, and asked if his daughter was possibly there?

"No, she's not, Mr. Skipperton."

"Is your son there? I'd like—"

"No, he doesn't happen to be in just now."

"What do you mean? He was there and went out?"

"Mr. Skipperton, my son has his own ways, his own room, his own key—his own life. I'm not about—"

Skipperton put the telephone down suddenly. He had a bad nosebleed, and it was dripping onto the table edge. He ran to get a wet towel.

Maggie was not home by Sunday evening or Monday morning, and Skipperton was reluctant to notify the police, appalled by the thought that her name might be linked with the Frosbys', if the police found her with the son somewhere. Tuesday morning, Skip was enlightened. He had a letter from Maggie, written from Boston. It said that she and Pete had run away to be married, and to avoid "unpleasant scenes."

> ...Though you may think this is sudden, we do love each
> other and are sure of it. I did not really want to go back
> to school, Daddy. I will be in touch in about a week.
> Please don't try to find me. I have seen Mommie, but we
> are not staying with her. I was sorry to leave my nice new
> car, but the car is all right.
>
> Love always,
Maggie

For two days Skipperton didn't go out of the house, and hardly ate. He felt three-quarters dead. Andy was very worried about him, and finally persuaded Skipperton to ride to the village with him, because they needed to buy a few things. Skipperton went, sitting like an upright corpse in the passenger seat.

While Andy went to the drugstore and the butcher's, Skipperton sat in the car, his eyes glazed with his own thoughts. Then an approaching figure on the sidewalk made Skipperton's eyes focus. Old Frosby! Frosby walked with a springy tread for his age, Skip thought. He wore a new tweed suit, black felt hat, and he had a cigar in his hand. Skipperton hoped Frosby wouldn't see him in the car, but Frosby did.

Frosby didn't pause in his stride, just smiled his obnoxious, thin-lipped little smile and nodded briefly, as if to say—

Well, Skip *knew* what Frosby might have wanted to say, what he had said with that filthy smile. Skip's blood seethed, and Skip began to feel like his old self again. He was standing on the sidewalk, hands in his pockets and feet apart, when Andy reappeared.

"What's for dinner tonight, Andy? I've got an appetite!"

That evening, Skipperton persuaded Andy to take not only Saturday night off, but to stay overnight somewhere, if he wished. "Give you a couple of hundred bucks for a little spree, boy. You've earned it." Skip forced three hundred dollar bills into Andy's hand. "Take off Monday too, if you feel like it. I'll manage."

Andy left Saturday evening in the pick-up for Bangor.

Skip then telephoned old Frosby. Frosby answered, and Skipperton said, "Mr. Frosby, it's time we made a truce, under the circumstances. Don't you think so?"

Frosby sounded surprised, but he agreed to come Sunday morning around eleven for a talk. Frosby arrived in the same Cadillac, alone.

And Skipperton wasted no time. He let Frosby knock, opened the door for him, and as soon as Frosby was inside, Skip came down on his head with a rifle butt. He dragged Frosby to the hall to make sure the job was finished: the hall was uncarpeted, and Skip wanted no blood on the rugs. Vengeance was sweet to Skip, and he almost smiled. He removed Frosby's clothes, and wrapped his body in three or four burlap sacks which he had ready. Then he burnt Frosby's clothing in the fireplace, where he had a small fire already crackling. Frosby's wristwatch and wallet and two rings Skip put aside in a drawer to deal with later.

He had decided that broad daylight was the best time to carry out his idea, better than night when an oddly playing flashlight that he would have had to use might have caught someone's eye. So Skip put one arm around Frosby's body and dragged him up the field towards his scarecrow. It was a haul of more than half a mile. Skip had some rope and a knife in his back pockets. He cut down the old scarecrow, cut the strings that held the clothing to the cross, dressed Frosby in the old trousers and jacket, tied a burlap bag around his head and face, and jammed the hat on him. The hat wouldn't stay without being tied on, so Skip did this after punching holes in the brim of the hat with his knife point. Then Skip picked up his burlap bags and made his way back towards his house down the slope with many a backward look to admire his work, and many a smile. The scarecrow looked almost the same as before. He had solved a problem a lot of people thought diffi- cult: what to do with the body. Furthermore, he could enjoy look- ing at it through his binoculars from his upstairs window.

Skip burnt the burlap bags in his fireplace, made sure that even the shoe soles had burnt to soft ash. When the ashes were cooler, he'd look for buttons and the belt buckle and remove them. He took a fork, went out beyond the pig run and buried the wallet (whose papers he had already burnt), the wristwatch and the rings about three feet deep. It was in a patch of stringy grass, unused for anything except the goats, not a place in which anyone would ever likely do any gardening.

Then Skip washed his face and hands, ate a thick slice of roast beef, and put his mind to the car. It was by now half past twelve. Skip didn't know if Frosby had a servant, someone expecting him for lunch or not, but it was safer to assume he had. Skip's aversion to Frosby had kept him from asking Maggie any questions about his household. Skip got into Frosby's car, now with a kitchen towel in his back pocket to wipe off fingerprints, and drove to some

woods he knew from having driven past them many times.
An unpaved lane went off the main road into these woods, and
into this Skip turned. Thank God, nobody in sight, not a woods-
man, not a picnicker. Skip stopped the car and got out, wiped the
steering wheel, even the keys, the door, then walked back towards
the road.

He was more than an hour getting home. He had found a
long stick, the kind called a stave by the wayfarers of old, Skip
thought, and he trudged along with the air of a nature-lover, a
bird-watcher, for the benefit of the people in the few cars that
passed him. He didn't glance at any of the cars. It was still Sunday
dinnertime.

The local police telephoned that evening around seven, and
asked if they could come by. Skipperton said of course.

He had removed the buttons and buckle from the fireplace
ashes. A woman had telephoned around 1:30, saying she was calling from the Frosby residence (Skip assumed she was a servant) to
ask if Mr. Frosby was there. Skipperton told her that Mr. Frosby
had left his house a little after noon.

"Mr. Frosby intended to go straight home, do you think?" the
plump policeman asked Skipperton. The policeman had some
rank like sergeant, Skipperton supposed, and he was accompanied
by a younger policeman.

"He didn't say anything about where he was going," Skipperton replied. "And I didn't notice which way his car went."

The policeman nodded, and Skip could see he was on the
brink of saying something like, "I understand from Mr. Frosby's
housekeeper that you and he weren't on the best of terms," but the
cop didn't say anything, just looked around Skip's living room,
glanced around his front and back yards in a puzzled way, then
both policemen took their leave.

Skip was awakened around midnight by the ring of the telephone at his bedside. It was Maggie calling from Boston. She and
Pete had heard about the disappearance of Pete's father.

"Daddy, they said he'd just been to see you this morning. What happened?"

"Nothing happened. I invited him for a friendly talk—and it was friendly. After all we're fathers-in-law now . . . Honey, how do I know where he went?"

Skipperton found it surprisingly easy to lie about Frosby. In a primitive way his emotions had judged, weighed the situation, and told Skip that he was right, that he had exacted a just revenge. Old Frosby might have exerted some control over his son, and he hadn't. It had cost Skip his daughter—because that was the way Skip saw it, Maggie was lost to him. He saw her as a provincial-to-be, mother-to-be of children whose narrow-mindedness, inherited from the Frosby clan, would surely out.

Andy arrived next morning, Monday. He had already heard the story in the village, and also the police had found Mr. Frosby's car not far away in the woods, Andy said. Skip feigned mild surprise on hearing of the car. Andy didn't ask any questions. And suppose he discovered the scarecrow? Skip thought a little money would keep Andy quiet. The corn was all picked up there, only a few inferior ears remained, destined for the pigs. Skipperton picked them himself Monday afternoon, while Andy tended the pigs and goats.

Skipperton's pleasure now was to survey the cornfield from his upstairs bedroom with his 10¥ binoculars. He loved to see the wind tossing the cornstalk tops around old Frosby's corpse, loved to think of him, shrinking, drying up like a mummy in the wind. Twisting slowly, slowly in the wind, as a Nixon aide used to put it about the president's enemies. Frosby wasn't twisting, but he was hanging, in plain view. No buzzards came. Skip had been a little afraid of buzzards. The only thing that bothered him, once, was seeing one afternoon some schoolboys walking along a road far to the right (under which road the Coldstream flowed), and pointing to the scarecrow. Bracing himself against the window jamb, arms held tightly at his sides so the binoculars would be as steady as possible, Skip saw a couple of the small boys laughing. And had one held his nose? Surely not! They were nearly a mile away from the scarecrow! Still, they had paused, one boy stamped his foot, another shook his head and laughed.

How Skip wished he could hear what they were saying! Ten days had passed since Frosby's death. Rumors were rife, that old Frosby had been murdered for his money by someone he'd picked up to give a lift to, that he had been kidnapped and that a ransom note might still arrive. But suppose one of the schoolkids said to his father—or anyone—that maybe the dead body of Frosby was inside the scarecrow? This was just the kind of thing Skip might have thought of when he had been a small boy. Skip was consequently more afraid of the schoolkids than of the police.

And the police did come back, with a plainclothes detective. They looked over Skipperton's house and land—maybe looking for a recently dug patch, Skip thought. If so, they found none. They looked at Skip's two rifles and took their caliber and serial numbers.

"Just routine, Mr. Skipperton," said the detective.

"I understand," said Skip.

That same evening Maggie telephoned and said she was at the Frosby house, and could she come over to see him?

"Why not? This is your house!" Skip replied.

"I never know what kind of mood you'll be in—or temper," Maggie said when she arrived.

"I'm in a pretty *good* mood, I think," Skipperton said. "And I hope you're happy, Maggie—since what's done is done."

Maggie was in her blue dungarees, sneakers, a familiar sweater. It was hard for Skip to realize that she was married. She sat with hands folded, looking down at the floor. Then she raised her eyes to him and said:

"Pete's very upset. We never would have stayed a week in Boston unless he'd been sure the police were doing all they could here. Was Mr. Frosby—depressed? Pete didn't think so."

Skip laughed. "No! Best of spirits. Pleased with the marriage and all that." Skip waited, but Maggie was silent. "You're going to live at the Frosby place?"

"Yes." Maggie stood up. "I'd like to collect a few things, Daddy. I brought a suitcase."

His daughter's coolness, her sadness, pained Skip. She had said something about visiting him often, not about his coming to see them—not that Skip would have gone.

"I KNOW WHAT'S in that scarecrow," said Andy one day, and Skip turned, binoculars in hand, to see Andy standing in the doorway of his bedroom.

"Do you?—And what're you going to do about it?" Skip asked, braced for anything. He had squared his shoulders.

"Nothin'. Nothin'," Andy replied with a smile.

Skip didn't know how to take that. "I suppose you'd like some money, Andy? A little present—for keeping quiet?"

"No, sir," Andy said quietly, shaking his head. His wind-wrinkled face bore a faint smile. "I ain't that kind."

What was Skip to make of it? He was used to men who liked money, more and more of it. Andy was different, that was true. Well, so much the better, if he didn't want money, Skip thought. It was cheaper. He also felt he could trust Andy. It was strange.

The leaves began to fall in earnest. Halloween was coming, and Andy removed the driveway gate in advance, just lifted it off its hinges, telling Skip that the kids would steal it if they didn't. Andy knew the district. The kids didn't do much harm, but it was trick or treat at every house. Skip and Andy made sure they had lots of nickels and quarters on hand, corn candy, licorice sticks, even a couple of pumpkins in the window, faces cut in them by Andy, to show any comers that they were in the right spirit. Then on Halloween night, nobody knocked on Skip's door. There was a party at Coldstream, at the Frosbys', Skip knew because the wind was blowing his way and he could hear the music. He thought of his daughter dancing, having a good time. Maybe people were wearing masks, crazy costumes. There'd be pumpkin pie with whipped cream, guessing games, maybe a treasure hunt. Skip was lonely, for the first time in his life. *Lonely.* He badly wanted a scotch, but decided to keep his oath to himself, and having decided this, asked himself why? He put his hands flat down on his dresser top and gazed at his own face in the mirror. He saw creases running from the flanges of his nose down beside his mouth, wrinkles under his eyes. He tried to smile, and the smile looked phony. He turned away from the mirror.

At that instant, a spot of light caught his eyes. It was out the window, in the upward sloping field. A procession—so it seemed, maybe eight or ten figures—was walking up his field with flashlights or torches or both. Skip opened the window slightly. He was rigid with rage, and fear. They were on his land! They had no right! And they were kids, he realized. Even in the darkness, he could see by the procession's own torches that the figures were a lot shorter than adults' figures would be.

Skip whirled around, about to shout for Andy, and at once decided that he had better not. He ran downstairs and grabbed his own powerful flashlight. He didn't bother grabbing his jacket from a hook, though the night was crisp.

"Hey!" Skip yelled, when he had run several yards into the field. "Get off my property! What're you *doing* walking up there!"

The kids were singing some crazy, high-pitched song, nobody singing on key. It was just a wild treble chant. Skip recognized the word "scarecrow."

"We're going to burn the scarecrow . . ." something like that.

"Hey, there! Off my land!" Skip fell, banged a knee, and scrambled up again. The kids had heard him, Skip was pretty sure, but they weren't stopping. Never before had anyone disobeyed Skip— except of course Maggie. *"Off my land!"*

The kids moved on like a black caterpillar with an orange headlight and a couple of other lights in its body. Certainly the last couple of kids had heard Skip, because he had seen them turn, then run to catch up with the others. Skip stopped running. The caterpillar was closer to the scarecrow than he was, and he was not going to be able to get there first.

Even as he thought this, a whoop went up. A scream! Another scream of mingled terror and delight shattered their chant. Hysteria broke out. What surely was a little girl's throat gave a cry as shrill as a dog whistle. Their hands must have touched the corpse, maybe touched bone, Skip thought.

Skip made his way back towards his own house, his flashlight pointed at the ground. It was worse than the police, somehow. Every kid was going to tell his parents what he had found. Skip knew he had come to the end. He had seen businessmen, seen a lot of men come to the end. He had known men who had jumped out of windows, who had taken overdoses.

Skip went at once to his rifle. It was in the living room downstairs. He put the muzzle in his mouth and pulled the trigger.

When the kids streaked down the field, heading for the road a few seconds later, Skip was dead. The kids had heard the shot, and thought someone was trying to shoot at them.

Andy heard the shot. He had also seen the procession marching up the field and heard Skipperton shouting. He understood what had happened. He turned his television set off, and made his way rather slowly towards the main house. He would have to call the police. That was the right thing to do. Andy made up his mind to say to the police that he didn't know a thing about the corpse in the scarecrow's clothes. He had been away some of that weekend after all.

Those Awful Dawns

Eddie's face looked angry and blank also, as if he might be thinking of something else. He was staring at his two-year-old daughter Francy who sat in a wailing heap beside the double bed. Francy had tottered to the bed, struck it, and collapsed.

"*You* take care of her," Laura said. She was standing with the vacuum cleaner still in her hand. "I've got things to do!"

"You hit her, f'Christ's sake, so *you* take care of her!" Eddie was shaving at the kitchen sink.

Laura dropped the vacuum cleaner, started to go to Francy, whose cheek was bleeding, changed her mind and veered back to the vacuum cleaner and unplugged it, began to wrap the cord to put it away. The place could stay a mess tonight for all she cared.

The other three children, Georgie nearly six, Helen four, Stevie three, stared with wet, faintly smiling mouths.

"That's a cut, goddamnit!" Eddie put a towel under the baby's cheek. "Swear to God, that'll need stitches. Lookit it! How'd you do it?"

Laura was silent, at least as far as answering that question went. She felt exhausted. The boys—Eddie's pals—were coming tonight at nine to play poker, and she had to make at least twenty liverwurst and ham sandwiches for their midnight snack. Eddie had slept all day and was still only getting dressed at 7 P.M.

"You taking her to the hospital or what?" Eddie asked. His face was half covered with shaving cream.

"If I take her again, they'll think it's always *you* smacking her. Mostly it is, frankly."

"Don't give me that crap, not this time," Eddie said. "And 'they,' who the hell're 'they'? Shove 'em!"

Twenty minutes later, Laura was in the waiting hall of St. Vincent's Hospital on West 11th Street. She leaned back in the straight chair and half closed her eyes. There were seven other people waiting, and the nurse had told her it might be half an hour, but she would try to make it sooner because the baby was bleeding slightly. Laura had her story ready: the baby had fallen against the vacuum cleaner, must've hit the connecting part where there was a sliding knob. Since this was what Laura had hit her with; swinging it suddenly to one side because Francy had been pulling at it, Laura supposed that the same injury could be caused by Francy's falling against it. That made sense.

It was the third time they'd brought Francy to St. Vincent's, which was four blocks from where they lived on Hudson Street. Broken nose (Eddie's fault, Eddie's elbow), then another time a trickling of blood at the ear that wouldn't stop, then the third time, the one time they hadn't brought her on their own, was when Francy had had a broken arm. Neither Eddie nor Laura had known Francy had a broken arm. How could they have known? You couldn't see it. But around that time Francy had had a black eye, God knew how or why, and a social worker had turned up. A neighbor must have put the social worker on their tail, and Laura was ninety percent sure it was old Mrs. Covini on the ground floor, damn her ass. Mrs. Covini was one of those dumpy, black-dressed Italian mommas who lived surrounded by kids all their lives, nerves of steel, who hugged and kissed the kids all day as if they were gifts from heaven and very rare things on earth. The Mrs. Covinis didn't go out to work, Laura had always noticed. Laura worked as a waitress five nights a week at a downtown Sixth Avenue diner. That plus getting up at 6 A.M. to fix Eddie's bacon and eggs, pack his lunchbox, feed the kids who were already up, and cope with them all day was enough to make an ox tired, wasn't it? Anyway, Mrs. Covini's spying had brought this monster—she was five feet eleven if she was an inch—down on their necks three times. Her name, appropriately enough, was Mrs. Crabbe. "Four children are a lot to handle . . . Are you in the habit of using contraceptives, Mrs. Regan?" Oh, crap. Laura moved her head from side to side on the back of the straight chair and groaned, feeling exactly as she had felt in high school when confronted by a problem in algebra that bored her stiff. She and Eddie were practicing Catholics. She might have been willing to go on the Pill on her own, but Eddie wouldn't hear of it, and that was that. On her own, that was funny, because on her own she wouldn't have needed it. Anyway, that had shut old Crabbe up on the subject, and had given Laura a certain satisfaction. She and Eddie had some rights and independence left, at least.

"Next?" The nurse beckoned, smiling.

The young intern whistled. "How'd this happen?"

"A fall. Against the vacuum cleaner."

The smell of disinfectant. Stitches. Francy, who had been nearly asleep in the hall, had awakened at the anesthetizing needle and wailed through the whole thing. The intern gave Francy what he called a mild sedative in a candy-covered pill. He murmured something to a nurse.

"What're these bruises?" he asked Laura. "On her arms."

"Oh—just bumps. In the house. She bruises easily." He wasn't the same intern, was he, that Laura had seen three or four months ago?

"Can you wait just a minute?"

The nurse came back, and she and the intern looked at a card that the nurse had.

The nurse said to Laura, "I think one of our OPTs is visiting you now, Mrs. Regan?"

"Yes."

"Have you an appointment with her?"

"Yes, I think so. It's written down at home." Laura was lying.

MRS. CRABBE ARRIVED at 7:45 P.M. the following Monday without warning. Eddie had just got home and opened a can of beer. He was a construction worker, doing overtime nearly every day in the summer months when the light lasted. When he got home he always made for the sink, sponged himself with a towel, opened a can of beer, and sat down at the oilcloth-covered table in the kitchen.

Laura had already fed the kids at 6 P.M., and had been trying to steer them to bed when Mrs. Crabbe arrived. Eddie had cursed on seeing her come in the door.

"I'm sorry to intrude . . ." Like hell. "How have you been doing?"

Francy's face was still bandaged, and the bandage was damp and stained with egg. The hospital had said to leave the bandage on and not touch it. Eddie, Laura and Mrs. Crabbe sat at the kitchen table, and it turned into quite a lecture.

". . . You realize, don't you, that you both are using little Frances as an outlet for your bad temper. Some people might bang their fists against a wall or quarrel with each other, but you and your husband are apt to whack baby Frances. Isn't that true?" She smiled a phony, friendly smile, looking from one to the other of them.

Eddie scowled and mashed a book of matches in his fingers. Laura squirmed and was silent. Laura knew what the woman meant. Before Francy had been born, they had used to smack Stevie maybe a little too often. They damned well hadn't wanted a third baby, especially in an apartment the size of this one, just as the woman was saying now. And Francy was the fourth.

". . . but if you both can realize that Francy is—here . . ."

Laura was glad that she apparently wasn't going to bring up birth control again. Eddie looked about to explode, sipping his beer as if he was ashamed to have been caught with it, but as if he had a right to drink it if he wanted to, because it was his house.

". . . a larger apartment, maybe? Bigger rooms. That would ease the strain on your nerves a lot . . ."

Eddie was obliged to speak about the economic situation. "Yeah, I earn fine . . . Riveter-welder. Skilled. But we got expenses, y'know. I wouldn't wanta go looking for a bigger place. Not just now."

Mrs. Crabbe lifted her eyes and stared around her. Her black hair was neatly waved, almost like a wig. "That's a nice TV. You bought that?"

"Yeah, and we're still paying on it. That's *one* of the things," Eddie said.

Laura was tense. There was also Eddie's hundred-and-fifty-dollar wristwatch they were paying on, and luckily Eddie wasn't wearing it now (he was wearing his cheap one), because he didn't wear the good one to work.

"And the sofa and the armchairs, aren't they new . . . You bought them?"

"Yeah," Eddie said, hitching back in his chair. "This place is furnished, y'know, but you shoulda seen that—" He made a derisive gesture in the direction of the sofa.

Laura had to support Eddie here. "What they had here, it was an old red plastic thing. You couldn't even sit on it." It hurt your ass, Laura might have added.

"When we move to a bigger place, at least we've got those," Eddie said, nodding at the sofa and armchairs section.

The sofa and armchairs were covered with beige plush that had a floral pattern of pale pink and blue. Hardly three months in the house, and the kids had already spotted the seats with chocolate milk and orange juice. Laura found it impossible to keep the kids off the furniture. She was always yelling at them to play on the floor. But the point was the sofa and the armchairs weren't paid for yet, and that was what Mrs. Crabbe was getting at, not people's comfort or the way the house looked, oh no.

"Nearly paid up. Finished next month," Eddie said.

That wasn't true. It would be another four or five months, because they'd twice missed the payments, and the man at the 14th Street store had come near taking the things away.

Now there was a speech from the old bag about the cost of installment-plan buying. Always pay the whole sum, because if you couldn't do that, you couldn't afford whatever it was, see? Laura smoldered, as angry as Eddie, but the important thing with these meddlers was to appear to agree with everything they said. Then they might not come back.

". . . if this keeps up with little Frances, the law will have to step in and I'm sure you wouldn't want that. That would mean taking Frances to live somewhere else."

The idea was quite pleasant to Laura.

"Where? Take'er where?" Georgie asked. He was in pajama pants, standing near the table.

Mrs. Crabbe paid him no mind. She was ready to leave.

Eddie gave a curse when she was out the door, and went to get another beer. "*Goddamn invasion of privacy!*" He kicked the fridge door shut.

Laura burst out in a laugh. "That old sofa! Remember? *Jesus!*"

"Too bad it wasn't here, she coulda broke her behind on it."

That night around midnight, as Laura was carrying a heavy tray of four superburgers and four mugs of coffee, she remembered something that she had put out of her mind for five days. Incredible that she hadn't thought of it for five whole days. Now it was more than ever likely. Eddie would blow his stack.

The next morning on the dot of nine, Laura called up Dr. Weebler from the newspaper store downstairs. She said it was urgent, and got an appointment for 11:15. As Laura left for the doctor's, Mrs. Covini was in the hall, mopping the part of the white tiles directly in front of her door. Laura thought that was somehow bad luck, seeing Mrs. Covini now. She and Mrs. Covini didn't speak to each other any more.

"I can't give you an abortion just like that," Dr. Weebler said, shrugging and smiling his awful smile that seemed to say, "It's you holding the bag. I'm a doctor, a man." He said, "These things can be prevented. Abortions shouldn't be necessary."

I'll damn well go to another doctor, Laura thought with rising anger, but she kept a pleasant, polite expression on her face. "Look, Dr. Weebler, my husband and I are practicing Catholics, I told you that. At least my husband is and—you know. So these things happen. But I've already got four. Have a heart."

"Since when do practicing Catholics want abortions? No, Mrs. Regan, but I can refer you to another doctor."

And abortions were supposed to be easy lately in New York. "If I get the money together—How much is it?" Dr. Weebler was cheap, that was why they went to him.

"It's not a matter of money." The doctor was restless. He had other people waiting to see him.

Laura wasn't sure of herself, but she said, "You do abortions on other women, so why not me?"

"*Who?*—When there's a danger to a woman's health, that's different."

Laura didn't get anywhere, and that useless expedition cost her $7.50, payable on the spot, except that she did get another prescription for half-grain Nembutals out of him. That night she told Eddie. Better to tell him right away than postpone it, because postponing it was hell, she knew from experience, with the damned subject crossing her mind every half hour.

"Oh, *Chr-r-rist!*" Eddie said, and fell back on the sofa, mashing the hand of Stevie who was on the sofa and had stuck out a hand just as Eddie plopped.

Stevie let out a wail.

"Oh, shut up, that didn't kill you!" Eddie said to Stevie. "Well, now what. Now what?"

Now what. Laura was actually trying to think *now what.* What the hell ever was there to do except hope for a miscarriage, which never happened. Fall down the stairs, something like that, but she'd never had the guts to fall down the stairs. At least not so far. Stevie's wailing was like awful background music. Like in a horror film. "Oh, can it, Stevie!"

Then Francy started yelling. Laura hadn't fed her yet.

"I'm gonna get drunk," Eddie announced. "I suppose there's no booze."

He knew there wasn't. There never was any booze, it got

drunk up too fast. Eddie was going to go out. "Don't you want to eat first?" Laura asked.

"Naw." He pulled on a sweater. "I just want to forget the whole damned thing. Just forget it for a *little* while."

Ten minutes later, after poking something at Francy (mashed potatoes, a nippled bottle because it made less mess than a cup) and leaving the other kids with a box of Fig Newtons, Laura did the same thing, but she went to a bar farther down Hudson where she knew he didn't go. Tonight was one of her two nights off from the diner, which was a piece of luck. She had two whiskey sours with a bottle of beer as accompaniment, and then a rather nice man started talking with her, and bought her two more whiskey sours. On the fourth, she was feeling quite wonderful, even rather decent and important sitting on the bar stool, glancing now and then at her reflection in the mirror behind the bottles. Wouldn't it be great to be starting over again? No marriage, no Eddie, no kids? Just something new, a clean slate.

"I asked you—are you married?"

"No," Laura said.

But apart from that, he talked about football. He had won a bet that day. Laura daydreamed. Yes, she'd once had a marriage, love and all that. She'd known Eddie would never make a lot of dough, but there was such a thing as living decently, wasn't there, and God knew her tastes weren't madly expensive, so what took all the money? The kids. There was the drain. Too bad Eddie was a Catholic, and when you marry a Catholic—

"Hey, you're not listening!"

Laura dreamed on with determination. Above all, she'd *had a dream* once, a dream of love and happiness and of making a nice home for Eddie and herself. Now the outsiders were even attacking her *inside her house.* Mrs. Crabbe. A lot Mrs. Crabbe knew about being waked up at five in the morning by a screaming kid, or being poked in the face by Stevie or Georgie when you'd been asleep only a couple of hours and your whole body ached. That was when she or Eddie was apt to swat them. In those awful dawns. Laura realized she was near tears, so she began to listen to the man who was still going on about football.

He wanted to walk her home, so she let him. She was so tipsy, she rather needed his arm. Then she said at the door that she lived with her mother, so she had to go up alone. He started getting fresh, but she gave him a shove and closed the front door, which locked. Laura hadn't quite reached the third floor when she heard feet on the stairs and thought the guy must've got in somehow, but it turned out to be Eddie.

"Well, how d'y'do?" said Eddie, feeling no pain.

The kids had got into the fridge. It was something they did about once a month. Eddie flung Georgie back and shut the fridge, then slipped on some spilled stringbeans and nearly fell.

"And lookit the *gas,* f'Christ's sake!" Eddie said.

Every burner was on, and as soon as Laura saw it, she smelled gas, gas everywhere. Eddie flipped all the burners shut and opened a window.

Georgie's wailing started all the others.

"Shut up, shut up!" Eddie yelled. "What the hell's the matter, are they hungry? Didn't you feed 'em?"

"Of course I fed 'em!" Laura said.

Eddie bumped into the door jamb, his feet slipped sideways in a funny slow motion collapse, and he sat down heavily on the floor. Four-year-old Helen laughed and clapped her hands. Stevie was giggling. Eddie cursed the entire household, and flung his sweater at the sofa, missing it. Laura lit a cigarette. She still had her whiskey sour buzz and she was enjoying it.

She heard the crash of a glass on the bathroom floor, and she merely raised her eyebrows and inhaled smoke. Got to tie Francy in her crib, Laura thought, and moved vaguely towards Francy to do it. Francy was sitting like a dirty rag doll in a corner. Her crib was in the bedroom, and so was the double bed in which the other three kids slept. Goddamn bedroom certainly was a bedroom,

Laura thought. Beds were all you could see in there. She pulled
Francy up by her tied-around bib, and Francy just then burped,
sending a curdled mess over Laura's wrist.

"Ugh!" Laura dropped the child and shook her hand with
disgust.

Francy's head had bumped the floor, and now she let out a
scream. Laura ran water over her hand at the sink, shoving aside
Eddie who was already stripped to the waist, shaving. Eddie shaved
at night so that he could sleep a little longer in the morning.

"You're pissed," Eddie said.

"And so what?" Laura went back and shook Francy to make
her hush. "For God's sake, shut up! What've *you* got to cry about?"

"Give'er an aspirin. Take some yourself," Eddie said.

Laura told him what to do with himself. If Eddie came at her
tonight, he could shove it. She'd go back to the bar. Sure. That
place stayed open till three in the morning. Laura found herself
pushing a pillow down on Francy's face to shut her up just for a
minute, and Laura remembered what Mrs. Crabbe had said: Francy
had become the target—Target? Outlet for both of them. Well, it
was true, they did smack Francy more than the others, but Francy
yelled more, too. Suiting action to the thought, Laura slapped
Francy's face hard. That's what they did when people had hyster-
ics, she thought. Francy did shut up, but for only a stunned couple
of seconds, then yelled even louder.

The people below were thumping on their ceiling. Laura
imagined them with a broom handle. Laura stamped three times
on her floor in defiance.

"Listen, if you don't get that kid *quiet*—" Eddie said.

Laura stood at the closet undressing. She pulled on a nightgown, and pushed her feet into old brown loafers that served as
house slippers. In the john, Eddie had broken the glass that they
used when they brushed their teeth. Laura kicked some of the glass
aside, too tired to sweep it up tonight. Aspirins. She took down a

bottle and it slipped from her fingers before she got the top unscrewed. Crash, and pills all over the floor. Yellow pills. The Nembutals. That was a shame, but sweep it all up tomorrow. Save them, the pills. Laura took two aspirins.

Eddie was yelling, waving his arms, herding the kids towards the other double bed. Usually that was Laura's job, and she knew Eddie was doing it because he didn't want them roaming around the house all night, disturbing him.

"And if you don't stay in that bed, all of yuh, I'll *wham* yuh!"

Thump-thump-thump on the floor again.

Laura fell into bed, and awakened to the alarm clock. Eddie groaned and moved slowly, getting out of bed. Laura lay savoring the last few seconds of bed before she would hear the clunk that meant Eddie had put the kettle on. She did the rest, instant coffee, orange juice, bacon and eggs, instant hot cereal for the kids. She went over last night in her mind. How many whiskey sours? Five, maybe, and only one beer. With the aspirins, that shouldn't be so bad.

"Hey, what's with Georgie?" Eddie yelled. "Hey, what the hell's in the john?"

Laura crawled out of bed, remembering. "I'll sweep it up."

Georgie was lying on the floor in front of the john door, and Eddie was stooped beside him.

"Aren't those Nembutals?" Eddie said. "Georgie musta ate some! And lookit Helen!"

Helen was in the bathroom, lying on the floor beside the shower.

Eddie shook Helen, yelling at her to wake up. "Jesus, they're like in a coma!" He dragged Helen out by an arm, picked Georgie up and carried him to the sink. He held Georgie under his arm like a sack of flour, wet a dishtowel and sloshed it over Georgie's face and head. "You think we oughta get a doctor?—F'Christ's sake, move, will yuh? Hand me Helen."

Laura did. Then she pulled on a dress. She kept the loafers on. She must phone Weebler. No, St. Vincent's, it was closer. "Do you remember the number of St. Vincent's?"

"No," said Eddie. "What d'y'do to make kids vomit? Anybody vomit? Mustard, isn't it?"

"Yeah, I think so." Laura went out the door. She still felt tipsy, and almost tripped on the stairs. Good thing if she did, she thought, remembering she was pregnant, but of course it never worked until you were pretty far gone.

She hadn't a dime with her, but the newspaper store man said he would trust her, and gave her a dime from his pocket. He was just opening, because it was early. Laura looked up the number, then in the booth she found that she had forgotten half of it. She'd have to look it up again. The newspaper store man was watching her, because she had said it was an emergency and she had to call a hospital. Laura picked up the telephone and dialed the number as best she remembered it. Then she put the forefinger of her right hand on the hook (the man couldn't see the hook), because she knew it wasn't the right number, but because the man was watching her, she started speaking. The dime was returned in the chute and she left it.

"Yes, please. An emergency." She gave her name and address. "Sleeping pills. I suppose we'll need a stomach pump . . . Thank you. Good-bye."

Then she went back to the apartment.

"They're still out cold," Eddie said. "How many pills're gone, do you think? Take a look."

Stevie was yelling for his breakfast. Francy was crying because she was still tied in her crib.

Laura took a look on the bathroom tiles, but she couldn't guess at all how many pills were gone. Ten? Fifteen? They were sugar-coated, that's why the kids had liked them. She felt blank, scared, and exhausted. Eddie had put the kettle on, and they had instant coffee, standing up. Eddie said there wasn't any mustard in the house (Laura remembered she had used the last of it for all

those ham sandwiches), and now he tried to get some coffee down
Georgie's and Helen's throats, but none seemed to go down, and
it only spilled on their fronts.

"Sweep up that crap so Stevie won't get any," Eddie said, nodding at the john. "What time're they coming? I gotta get going.
That foreman's a shit, I told you, he don't want nobody late." He
cursed, having picked up his lunchbox and found it empty, and he
tossed the lunchbox with a clatter in the sink.

Still dazed, Laura fed Francy at the kitchen table (she had
another black eye, where the hell did *that* come from?), started to
feed cornflakes and milk to Stevie (he wouldn't eat hot cereal), then
left it for Stevie to do, whereupon he turned the bowl over on the
oilcloth table. Georgie and Helen were still asleep on the double
bed where Eddie had put them. *Well, after all St. Vincent's is coming,*
Laura thought. But they weren't coming. She turned on the little
battery radio to some dance music. Then she changed Francy's diaper. That was what Francy was howling about, her wet diaper. Laura
had barely heard the howling this morning. Stevie had toddled over
to Georgie and Helen and was poking them, trying to wake them
up. In the john, Laura emptied the kids' pot down the toilet, washed
the pot out, swept up the broken glass and the pills, and picked the
pills out of the dustpan. She put the pills on a bare place on one of
the glass shelves in the medicine cabinet.

At ten, Laura went down to the newspaper store, paid the man
back, and had to look up the St. Vincent number again. This time
she dialed it, got someone, told them what was the matter and
asked why no one had come yet.

"You phoned at seven? That's funny. I was on. We'll send an
ambulance right away."

Laura bought four quarts of milk and more baby food at the
delicatessen, then went back upstairs. She felt a little less sleepy, but
not much. Were Georgie and Helen still breathing? She absolutely
didn't want to go and see. She heard the ambulance arriving. Laura
was finishing her third cup of coffee. She glanced at herself in the

mirror, but couldn't face that either. The more upset she looked, the better, maybe. Two men in white came up, and went at once to the two kids. They had stethoscopes. They murmured and exclaimed. One turned and asked:

"*Whad* they take?"

"Sleeping pills. They got into the Nembutals."

"This one's even cold. Didn't you notice that?"

He meant Georgie. One of the men wrapped the kids up in blankets from the bed, the other prepared a needle. He gave shots in the arm to both kids.

"No use telephoning us for another two three hours," one of them said.

The other said, "Never mind, she's in a state of shock. Better have some hot tea, lady, and lie down."

They hurried off. The ambulance whined towards St. Vincent's.

The whine was taken up by Francy, who was standing with her fat little legs apart, but no more apart than usual, while pee dripped from the lump of diaper between them. All the rubber pants were still dirty in the pan under the sink. It was a chore she should have done last night. Laura went over and smacked her on the cheek, just to shut her up for a minute, and Francy fell on the floor. Then Laura gave her a kick in the stomach, something she'd never done before. Francy lay there, silent for once.

Stevie stared wide-eyed and gaping, looking as if he didn't know whether to laugh or cry. Laura kicked her shoes off and went to get a beer. Naturally, there wasn't any. Laura combed her hair, then went down to the delicatessen. When she came back, Francy was sitting where she had lain before, and crying again. Change the diaper again? Stick a pair of dirty rubber pants on her? Laura opened a beer, drank some, then changed the diaper just to be doing something. Still with the beer beside her, she filled the sink with sudsy water and dumped the six pairs of rubber pants into it, and a couple of rinsed-out but filthy diapers as well.

The doorbell rang at noon, and it was Mrs. Crabbe, damn her eyes, just about as welcome as the cops.

This time Laura was insolent. She interrupted the old bitch every time she spoke. Mrs. Crabbe was asking how the children came to get at the sleeping pills? What time had they eaten them?

"I don't know why any human being has to put up with intrusions like this!" Laura yelled.

"Do you realize that your son is dead? He was bleeding internally from glass particles."

Laura let fly one of Eddie's favorite curses.

Then the old bag left the house, and Laura drank her beer, three cans of it. She was thirsty. When the bell rang again, she didn't answer it, but soon there was a knocking on the door. After a few minutes, Laura got so tired of it, she opened the door. It was old Crabbe again with two men in white, one carrying a satchel. Laura put up a fight, but they got a straitjacket on her. They took her to another hospital, not St. Vincent's. Here two people held her while a third person gave her a needle. The needle nearly knocked her out, but not quite.

That was how, one month later, she got her abortion. The most blessed event that ever happened to her.

She had to stay in the place—Bellevue—all that time. When she told the shrinks she was really fed up with marriage, her marriage, they seemed to believe her and to understand, yet they admitted to her finally that all their treatment was designed to make her go back to that marriage. Meanwhile, the three kids— Helen had recovered—were in some kind of free nursery. Eddie had come to see her, but she didn't want to see him, and thank God they hadn't forced her to. Laura wanted a divorce, but she knew Eddie would never say yes to a divorce. He thought people just didn't get divorced. Laura wanted to be free, independent, and alone. She didn't want to see the kids, either.

"I want to make a new life," she said to the psychiatrists, who had become as boring as Mrs. Crabbe.

The only way to get out of the place was to fool them, Laura realized, so she began to humor them, gradually. She would be allowed to go, they said, on condition that she went back to Eddie. But she wrung from a doctor a signed statement—she insisted on having it in writing—that she was to have no more children, which effectively meant that she had a right to take the Pill.

Eddie didn't like that, even if it was a doctor's orders. "That's not marriage," Eddie said.

Eddie had found a girlfriend while she was in Bellevue, and some nights he didn't come home, and went to work from wherever he was sleeping. Laura hired a detective for just one day, and discovered the woman's name and address. Then Laura sued for divorce on the grounds of adultery, no alimony asked, real Women's Lib. Eddie got the kids, which was fine with Laura because he wanted them more than she did. Laura got a full-time job in a department store, which was a bit tough, standing on her feet for so many hours, but all in all not so tough as what she had left. She was only twenty-five, and quite nice looking if she took the time to do her face and dress properly. There were good chances of advancement in her job, too.

"I feel peaceful now," Laura said to a new friend to whom she had told her past. "I feel different, as if I've lived a hundred years, and yet I'm still pretty young . . . Marriage? No, never again."

SHE WOKE UP and found it was all a dream. Well, not *all* a dream. The awakening was gradual, not a sudden awareness as in the morning when you open your eyes and see what's really in front of you. She'd been taking two kinds of pills on the doctor's orders. Now it seemed to her that the pills had been trick pills, to make the world seem rosy, to make her more cheerful—but really to get her to walk back into the same trap, like a doped sheep. She found herself standing at the sink on Hudson Street with a dishtowel in her hands. It was morning. 10:22 by the clock by the bed. But she *had* been to Bellevue, hadn't she? And Georgie had died, because now in the apartment there were only Stevie and Helen and Francy. It was September, she saw by a newspaper that was lying on the kitchen table. And—where was it? The piece of paper the doctor had signed?

Where did she keep it, in her billfold? She looked and it wasn't there. She unzipped the pocket in her handbag. Not there either. But she'd had it. Hadn't she? For an instant, she wondered if she was pregnant, but there wasn't a sign of it at her waistline. Then she went as if drawn by a mysterious force, a hypnotist's force, to a bruised brown leather box where she kept necklaces and bracelets. In this box was a tarnished old silver cigarette case big enough for only four cigarettes, and inside this was a folded piece of crisp white paper. That was it. She had it.

She went into the bathroom and looked into the medicine cabinet. What did they look like? There was something called Ovral. That must be it, it sounded sort of eggy. Well, at least she was taking them, the bottle was half empty. And Eddie was annoyed. She remembered now. But he had to put up with it, that was all.

But she hadn't tracked down his girlfriend with a detective. She hadn't had the job in the department store. Funny, when it was all so clear, that job, selling bright scarves and hosiery, making up her face so she looked great, making new friends. Had Eddie had a girlfriend? Laura simply wasn't sure. Anyway, he had to put up with the Pill now, which was one small triumph for her. But it didn't quite make up for what she had to put up with. Francy was crying. Maybe it was time to feed her.

Laura stood in the kitchen, biting her underlip, thinking she had to feed Francy now—food always shut her up a little—and thinking she'd have to start thinking hard, now that she could think, now that she was fully awake. Good God, life couldn't just go on like this, could it? She'd doubtless lost the job at the diner, so she'd have to find another, because they couldn't make it on Eddie's pay alone. *Feed Francy.*

The doorbell rang. Laura hesitated briefly, then pushed the release button. She had no idea who it was.

Francy yelled.

"All *right!*" Laura snapped, and headed for the fridge.

A knock on the door.

Laura opened the door. It was Mrs. Crabbe.

Woodrow Wilson's Necktie

The façade of Madame Thibault's Waxwork Horrors glittered and throbbed with red and yellow lights, even in the daytime. Golden balls like knobs—the yellow lights—pulsated amid the red lights, attracting the eye, holding it.

Clive Wilkes loved the place, the inside and outside equally. Since he was a delivery boy for a grocery store, it was easy for him to say a certain delivery had taken him longer than might be expected—he'd had to wait for Mrs. So-and-so to get home, because the doorman had told him she was due any minute, or he'd had to go five blocks to find some change, because Mrs. Zilch had had only a fifty-dollar bill. At these spare moments, and Clive found one or two a week, he visited Madame Thibault's Waxwork Horrors.

Inside the establishment, you went through a dark passage to get in the mood, and then you were confronted by a bloody murder scene: a girl with long blonde hair was sticking a knife into the neck of an old man who sat at a kitchen table eating his dinner. His dinner was a couple of wax frankfurters and wax sauerkraut. Then came the Lindbergh kidnapping, with Hauptmann climbing down a ladder outside a nursery window. You could see the top of the ladder outside the window, and the top half of Hauptmann's figure, clutching the little boy. Also there was Marat in his bath with Charlotte nearby. And Christie with his stocking throttlings of women. Clive loved every tableau, and they never became stale. But he didn't look at them with the solemn, vaguely startled expression of the other people who looked at them. Clive was inclined to smile, even to laugh. They were amusing. Why not laugh? Farther on in the museum were the torture chambers— one old, one modern, purporting to show twentieth-century torture methods in Nazi Germany and in French Algeria. Madame Thibault—who Clive strongly suspected did not exist—kept up to date. There were the Kennedy assassinations, of course, the Tate massacre, and as like as not a murder that had happened just a month ago somewhere.

Clive's first definite ambition in regard to Madame Thibault's Waxwork Horrors was to spend a night there. This he did one night, providently taking along a cheese sandwich in his pocket. It was fairly easy to accomplish. Clive knew that three people worked in the museum proper, down in the bowels as he thought of it, though the museum was on street level, while another man, a plumpish middle-aged fellow in a nautical cap, sold tickets out in front at a booth. There were two men and a woman who worked in the bowels. The woman, also plump with curly brown hair and glasses and about forty, took the tickets at the end of the dark corridor, where the museum began. One of the men lectured constantly, though not more than half the people ever bothered to listen. "Here we see the fanatical expression of the true murderer, captured by the wax artistry of Madame Thibault . . . blah-blah-blah . . ." The other man had black hair and black-rimmed glasses, and he just drifted around, shooing away kids who wanted to climb into the tableaux, maybe watching for pickpockets, or maybe protecting women from unpleasant assaults in the semi-darkness of the place, Clive didn't know.

He only knew it was quite easy to slip into one of the dark corners or into a nook next to one of the Iron Molls—maybe even into one of the Iron Molls, but slender as he was, the spikes might poke him, Clive thought, so he ruled out this idea. He had observed that people were gently urged out around 9:15 P.M. as the museum closed at 9:30 P.M. And lingering as late as possible one evening, Clive had learned that there was a sort of cloak room for the staff behind a door in one back corner, from which he had also heard the sound of a toilet flushing.

So one night in November, Clive concealed himself in the shadows, which were abundant, and listened to the three people as they got ready to leave. The woman—whose name seemed to be Mildred—was lingering to take the money box from Fred, the ticket-seller, and to count it and deposit it somewhere in the cloak room. Clive was not interested in the money, at least not very interested. He was interested in spending a night in the place, to be able to say that he had.

"Night, Mildred! See you tomorrow!" called one of the men.

"Anything else to do? I'm leaving now," said Mildred. "Boy, am I tired! But I'm still going to watch Dragon Man tonight."

"Dragon Man," the other man repeated, uninterested.

Evidently the ticket-seller Fred left from the front of the building after handing in the money box, and in fact Clive recalled seeing him close up the front once, cutting the lights from inside the entrance door, locking it.

Clive stood in a nook by an Iron Moll. When he heard the back door shut, and the key turn in the lock, he waited for a moment in delicious silence, aloneness, and suspense, then ventured out. He went first on tiptoe to the room where they kept their coats, because he had never seen it. He had brought matches (also cigarettes, though smoking was not allowed, according to several signs), and with the aid of a match, he found the light switch. The room contained an old desk, four or five metal lockers, a tin wastebasket, an umbrella stand, and some books in a bookcase against a rather grimy wall that had once been white. Clive slid open a drawer or two, and found the well-worn wooden box which he had once seen the ticket-seller carrying in through the front door. The box was locked. He could walk out with the box, he thought, but in fact he didn't care to, and he considered this rather decent of himself. He gave the box a wipe with the side of his hand, not forgetting the bottom where his fingertips had touched. That was funny, he thought, wiping something he hadn't stolen.

Clive set about enjoying the night. He found the lights, and put them on, so that the booths with the gory tableaux were all illuminated. He was hungry, and took one bite of his sandwich and put it back in the paper napkin in his pocket. He sauntered slowly past the John F. Kennedy assassination—Robert, Jackie, doctors bending anxiously over the white table on which JFK lay, leaking an ocean of blood which covered the floor. This time Haupt-mann's descent of the ladder made Clive giggle. Charles Lindbergh Jr.'s face looked so untroubled, one might have thought he was sit-ting on the floor of his nursery playing with blocks. Clive swung a leg over a metal bar and climbed into the Judd-Snyder fracas. It gave him a thrill to be standing right *with* them, inches from the throttling-from-behind which the lover was administering to the husband. Clive put a hand out and touched the red-paint blood that was beginning to come from the man's throat where the wire pressed. Clive also touched the cool cheekbones of the victim. The popping eyes were of glass, vaguely disgusting, and Clive did not touch those.

Two hours later, he was singing a church hymn, "Nearer My God to Thee" and "Jesus Wants Me for a Sunbeam." Clive didn't know all the words. He smoked.

By 2 A.M. he was bored, and tried to get out by both front door and back, but couldn't. No spare keys anywhere that he could find. He'd thought of having a hamburger at an all-night place between here and home. His incarceration didn't bother him, however, so he finished the now dry cheese sandwich, made use of the toilet, and slept for a bit on three straight chairs which he arranged in a row. It was so uncomfortable, he knew he would wake up in a while, which he did at 5 A.M. He washed his face, and went for another look at the wax exhibits. This time he took a souvenir—Woodrow Wilson's necktie.

As the hour of nine approached—Madame Thibault's Wax-work Horrors opened at 9:30 A.M.—Clive hid himself in an excel-lent spot, behind one of the tableaux whose backdrop was a black and gold Chinese screen. In front of the screen was a bed and in the bed lay a wax man with a handlebar mustache, who was sup-posed to be dead from poisoning by his wife.

The public began trickling in shortly after 9:30 A.M., and the taller, solemn man began mumbling his boring lecture. Clive had to wait till a few minutes past ten before he felt safe enough to mingle with the crowd and make his exit, with Woodrow Wilson's necktie rolled up in his pocket. He was a bit tired, but happy. Though on second thought, who would he tell about it? Joey Vrasky, that blond idiot who worked behind the counter at Simmons's Grocery? Hah! Why bother? Joey didn't deserve a good story. Clive was half an hour late for work.

"I'm sorry, Mr Simmons, I overslept," Clive said hastily, but he thought quite politely, as he came into the store. There was a delivery job awaiting him. Clive took his bicycle and put the box in front of the handlebars on a platform which had a curb, so a box would not fall off.

Clive lived with his mother, a thin, highly strung woman who was a saleswoman in a shop that sold stockings, girdles and underwear. Her husband had left her when Clive was five. She had no other children but Clive. Clive had quit high school a year before graduating, to his mother's regret, and for a year he had done nothing but lie around the house or stand on street corners with his chums. But Clive had never been very chummy with any of his friends, for which his mother was thankful, as she considered them a worthless lot. Clive had had the delivery job at Simmons's for nearly a year now, and his mother felt that he was settling down.

When Clive came home that evening at 6:30 P.M., he had a story ready for his mother. Last night he had run into his old friend Richie, who was in the army and home on leave, and they had sat up at Richie's talking so late, that Richie's parents had invited him to stay, and Clive had slept on the couch. His mother accepted this explanation. She made a supper of beans, bacon and eggs.

There was really no one to whom Clive felt like telling his exploit of the night. He couldn't have borne someone looking at him and saying, "Yeah? Well, so what?" because what he had done had taken a bit of planning, even a little daring. He put Woodrow Wilson's tie among his others that hung over a string on the inside of his closet door. It was a gray silk tie, conservative and expensive.

Several times that day, Clive imagined the two men in the place, or maybe the woman named Mildred, glancing at Woodrow Wilson and exclaiming:

"Hey! What happened to Woodrow Wilson's tie, I wonder?"

Each time Clive thought of this, he had to duck his head to hide his smile.

After twenty-four hours, however, the exploit had begun to lose its charm and excitement. Clive's excitement arose only again—and it could arise every day and two or three times a day—when he cycled past the twinkling façade of Madame Thibault's Waxwork Horrors. His heart would give a leap, his blood would run a little faster, and he would think of all the motionless murders going on in there, and all the stupid faces of Mr. and Mrs. Johnny Q. Public gaping at them. But Clive didn't even buy another ticket—price sixty-five cents—to go in and look at Woodrow Wilson and see that his tie was missing and his collar button showing—his work.

Clive did get another idea one afternoon, a hilarious idea that would make the public sit up and take notice. Clive's ribs trembled with suppressed laughter as he pedaled towards Simmons's, having just delivered a carton of groceries.

When should he do it? Tonight? No, best to take a day or so to plan it. It would take brains. And silence. And sure movements—all the things Clive admired. He spent two days thinking about it. He went to his local snack bar and drank Coca-Cola and beer, and played the pinball machines with his pals. The pinball machines had pulsating lights, too—MORE THAN ONE CAN PLAY and IT'S MORE FUN TO COMPETE—but Clive thought only of Madame Thibault's as he stared at the rolling, bouncing balls that mounted a score he cared nothing about. It was the same when he looked at the rainbow-colored jukebox whose blues, reds and yellows undulated, and when he went over to drop a few coins in it. He was thinking of what he was going to do in Madame Thibault's Waxwork Horrors.

On the second night, after a supper with his mother, Clive went to Madame Thibault's and bought a ticket. The old guy who sold tickets barely looked at people, he was so busy making change and tearing off tickets, which was just as well. Clive went in at 9 P.M.

He looked at the tableaux, though they were not so fascinating to him tonight as usual. Woodrow Wilson's tie was still missing, as if no one had noticed it, and Clive had a good chuckle over this, which he concealed behind his hand. Clive remembered that the solemn-faced pickpocket-watcher—the drifting snoop—had been the last to leave the night Clive had stayed, so Clive assumed he had the keys, and therefore he ought to be the last to be killed.

The woman was the first. Clive hid himself beside one of the Iron Molls again, while the crowd oozed out, and as Mildred walked past him, in her hat and coat, to leave via the back door, Clive stepped out and wrapped an arm around her throat from behind.

She made only a small "Ur–rk" sound.

Clive squeezed her throat with his hands, stopping her voice. At last she slumped, and Clive dragged her into a dark, recessed corner to the left of the cloakroom as one faced that room, and he knocked an empty cardboard box of some kind over, but it didn't make enough noise to attract the attention of the other two men.

"Mildred's gone?" one of the men said.

"She might be still in the office."

"No, she's not." This voice had already gone into the corridor where Clive crouched over Mildred, and had looked into the empty cloakroom where the light was still on. "She's left. Well, I'm calling it a day, too."

Clive stepped out then, and encircled this man's neck in the same manner. The job was more difficult, because the man struggled, but Clive's arm was thin and strong, he acted with swiftness, and he knocked the man's head against the nearest wall.

"What's going on?" The thump had brought the second man. This time, Clive tried a punch to the man's jaw, but missed and hit his neck. However, this so stunned the man—the solemn fellow, the snoop—that a second blow was easy, and then Clive was able to take him by the shirtfront and bash his head against the wall which was harder than the wooden floor. Then Clive made sure all three were dead. The two men's heads were bleeding. The woman was bleeding slightly from the mouth. Clive reached for the keys in the second man's pockets. They were in his left trousers pocket and with them was a penknife. Clive took the knife also.

Then the taller man moved slightly. Alarmed, Clive opened the pearl-handled penknife and went to work with it. He plunged it into the man's throat three or four times.

Close call! Clive thought, and he checked again to make sure they were all dead now. They most certainly were, and that was most certainly real blood coming out, not the red paint of Madame Thibault's Waxwork Horrors. Clive switched on the lights for the tableaux, and went into the exhibition hall for the interesting task of choosing the right places for the corpses.

The woman belonged in Marat's bath, not much doubt about that, and Clive debated removing her clothing, but decided against it, simply because she would look much funnier sitting in a bath with a fur-trimmed coat and hat on than naked. The figure of Marat sent him off in laughter. He'd expected sticks for legs, and nothing between the legs, because you couldn't see any more of Marat than from the middle of his torso up, but Marat had no legs at all, and his wax body ended just below the waist in a fat stump which was planted on a wooden platform so it would not topple. This crazy item Clive carried into the cloakroom and set squarely in the middle of the desk, like a Buddha. He then carried Mildred—who weighed a good bit—onto the Marat scene and stuck her in the bath. Her hat fell off and he pushed it on again, a bit over one eye. Her bleeding mouth hung open.

God, it *was* funny!

Now for the men. Obviously, the one whose throat he had cut would look good in the place of the old man who was eating franks and sauerkraut, because the girl behind him was supposed to be stabbing him in the throat. This work took Clive some fifteen minutes. Since the wax figure of the old man was in a seated position, Clive stuck him on the toilet off the cloakroom. It was amusing to see the old man on the toilet, throat bleeding, a knife in one hand and a fork in the other, apparently waiting for something to eat. Clive lurched against the doorjamb laughing loudly, not even caring if someone heard him, because it was so ludicrous, it was worth getting caught for.

Next, the little snoop. Clive looked around him, and his eye fell on the Woodrow Wilson scene, which depicted the signing of the armistice in 1918. A wax figure—Woodrow Wilson—sat at a huge desk signing a paper, and that was the logical place for a man whose head was split open and bleeding. With some difficulty Clive got the pen out of Woodrow Wilson's fingers, laid it to one side on the desk, and carried the figure—they did not weigh very much—into the cloakroom where Clive seated him at the desk, rigid arms in attitude of writing, and Clive stuck a ballpoint pen into his right hand. Now for the last heave. Clive saw that his jacket was now quite spotted with blood, and he would have to get rid of it, but so far no blood was on his trousers.

Clive dragged the second man to the Woodrow Wilson tableau, heaved him up onto the platform, and rolled him towards the desk. His head was still leaking blood. Clive got him up onto the chair, but the head toppled forward onto the green-blottered desk, onto the phony blank pages, and the pen barely stood upright in the limp hand.

But it was done. Clive stood back and smiled. Then he listened. Clive sat down on a straight chair somewhere and rested for a few minutes, because his heart was beating fast, and he suddenly realized that every muscle in his body was tired. Ah, well, now he had the keys. He could get out, go home, have a good night's rest, because he wanted to be ready to enjoy tomorrow. Clive took a sweater from one of the male figures in a log cabin tableau. He had to pull the sweater down over the feet to get it off, because the arms would not bend, and it stretched the neck of the sweater but that couldn't be helped. Now the wax figure had a bib of a shirt-front, and naked arms and chest.

Clive wadded up his jacket and went everywhere with it, eras-ing fingerprints wherever he thought he had touched. He turned the lights off, and made his way carefully to the back door, which was not locked. Clive locked it behind him, and would have left the keys in a mailbox, if there had been one, but there was none, so he dropped the keys on the doorstep. In a wire rubbish basket, he found some newspapers, and he wrapped his jacket in them, and walked on with it until he found another wire rubbish basket, where he forced the bundle down among candy wrappers and beer cans.

"A new sweater?" his mother asked that night.

"Richie gave it to me—for luck."

Clive slept like the dead, too tired even to laugh again at the memory of the old man sitting on the toilet.

The next morning, Clive was standing across the street when the ticket-seller arrived just before 9:30 A.M. By 9:35 A.M., only three people had gone in (evidently Fred had a key to the front door, in case his colleagues were late), but Clive could not wait any longer, so he crossed the street and bought a ticket. Now the ticket-seller was doubling as ticket-taker, or telling people, "Just go on in. Everybody's late this morning." The ticket man stepped inside the door to put on some lights, then walked all the way into the place to put on the display lights, which worked from switches in the hall that led to the cloakroom. And the funny thing to Clive, who was walking behind him, was that the ticket man didn't notice anything odd, didn't notice Mildred in hat and coat sitting in Marat's bathtub.

The customers so far were a man and woman, a boy of four-teen or so in sneakers, and a single man. They looked expression-lessly at Mildred in the tub, as if they thought it quite "normal," which could have sent Clive into paroxysms of mirth, except that his heart was thumping madly, and he was hardly breathing for suspense. Also, the man with his face in franks and sauerkraut brought no surprise either. Clive was a bit disappointed.

Two more people came in, a man and a woman.

Then at last by the Woodrow Wilson tableau, there was a reaction. One of the women clinging to a man's arm, asked:

"Was there someone shot when the armistice was signed?"

"I don't know. I don't *think* so," the man replied vaguely. "Yes-s—Let me think."

Clive's laughter pressed like an explosion in his chest, he spun on his heel to control himself, and he had the feeling he knew all about history, and that no one else did. By now, of course, the real blood had turned dark red. The green blotter was now dark red, and blood had run down the side of the desk.

A woman on the other side of the hall, where Mildred was, let out a scream.

A man laughed, but only briefly.

Suddenly everything happened. A woman shrieked, and at the same time, a man yelled, "My God, it's *real!*"

Clive saw a man climbing up to investigate the corpse with its face in the frankfurters.

"The blood's *real!* It's a dead *man!*"

Another man—one of the public—slumped to the floor. He had fainted!

The ticket-seller came bustling in. "What's the trouble?"

"Coupla corpses here! *Real* ones!"

Now the ticket-seller looked at Marat's bathtub and fairly jumped into the air with surprise. "Holy Christmas! Holy *cripes!*— *Mildred!*"

"And this one!"

"And the one here!"

"My God, got to—got to call the police!" said the ticket-seller Fred. "Could you all, please—just leave?"

One man and woman went out hurriedly. But the rest lingered, shocked, fascinated.

Fred had trotted into the cloakroom, where the telephone was, and Clive heard him yell something. He'd seen the man at the desk, of course, Woodrow Wilson, and Marat on the desk.

Clive thought it was time to drift out, so he did, sidling his way through four or five people who were peering in the door, coming in maybe because there was no ticket-seller.

That was good, Clive thought. That was all right. Not bad.

He had not intended to go to work that day, but suddenly he thought it wiser to check in and ask for the day off. Mr Simmons was of course as sour as ever when Clive said he was not feeling well, but as Clive held his stomach and appeared weak, there was little old Simmons could do. Clive left the store. He had brought with him all his ready cash, about twenty-three dollars.

Clive wanted to take a long bus ride somewhere. He realized that suspicion was likely to fall on him, if the ticket-seller remembered his coming to Madame Thibault's very often, or especially if he remembered his being there last night, but this had little to do with his desire to take a bus ride. His longing for a bus ride was simply, somehow, irresistible and purposeless. He bought a ticket westward for something over seven dollars, one way. This brought him, by about 7 P.M., to a good-sized town in Indiana, whose name Clive paid no attention to.

The bus spilled a few passengers, Clive included, at a terminal where there was a cafeteria and a bar. Clive by now was curious about the newspapers, and went at once to the newsstand near the street door of the cafeteria. And there it was:

TRIPLE MURDER IN WAXWORKS

MASS MURDER IN WAXWORKS MUSEUM

MYSTERY KILLER: THREE DEAD IN WAXWORKS MUSEUM

Clive liked the last headline best. He bought the three newspapers, and stood at the bar with a beer.

This morning at 9:30 A.M., ticket man Fred J. Keating and
several of the public who had come to see Madame
Thibault's Waxworks Horrors, a noted attraction of this
city, were confronted by three genuine corpses among the
displays. They were the bodies of Mrs. Mildred Veery, 41;
George P. Hartley, 43; and Richard K. MacFadden, 37, all
employed at the waxworks museum. The two men were
killed by concussions to the head, and in the case of one
also by stabbing, and the woman by strangulation. Police
are searching for clues on the premises. The murders are
believed to have taken place shortly before 10 P.M. last
evening, when the three employees were about to leave
the museum. The murderer or murderers may have been
among the last patrons of the museum before closing time
at 9:30 P.M. It is thought that he or they may have concealed themselves somewhere in the museum until the
rest of the patrons had left . . .

Clive was pleased. He smiled as he sipped his beer. He hunched
over the papers, as if he did not wish the rest of the world to share
his pleasure, but this was not true. After a few minutes, Clive looked
to right and left to see if anyone else among the men and a few
women at the bar were reading the story also. Two men were reading newspapers, but Clive could not tell if they were reading about
him necessarily, because their newspapers were folded. Clive lit a
cigarette and went through all three newspapers to see if there was
any clue about him. He found none at all. One paper said specifi-
cally that Fred J. Keating had not noticed any person or persons
entering the museum last evening who looked suspicious.

. . . Because of the bizarre arrangement of the victims and
of the displaced wax figures in the exhibitions, in whose
places the victims were put, police are looking for a psychopathic killer. Residents of the area have been warned
by radio and television to take special precautions on the
street and to keep their homes locked . . .

Clive chuckled over that one. Psychopathic killer. He was
sorry about the lack of detail, the lack of humor in the three
write-ups. They might have said something about the old guy sitting on the toilet. Or the fellow signing the armistice with the
back of his head bashed in. Those were strokes of genius. Why
didn't they appreciate them?

When he had finished his beer, Clive walked out onto the
sidewalk. It was now dark and the streetlights were on. He enjoyed
looking around in the new town, looking into shop windows. But
he was aiming for a hamburger place, and he went into the first
one he came to. It was a diner made up to look like a crack train
made of chromium. Clive ordered two hamburgers and a cup of
coffee. Next to him were two Western-looking men in cowboy
boots and rather soiled broad-brimmed hats. Was one a sheriff,
Clive wondered? But they were talking, in a drawl, about acreage
somewhere. Land. Money. They were hunched over hamburgers
and coffee, one so close his elbow kept brushing Clive's. Clive was
reading his newspapers all over again, and he had propped one
against the napkin container in front of him.

One of the men asked for a napkin and disturbed Clive, but
Clive smiled, and said in a friendly way:

"Did you read about the murders in the waxworks?"

The man looked blank, then said, "Saw the headlines."

"Someone killed the three people who worked in the place.
Look." There was a photograph in one of the papers, but Clive
didn't much like it, because it showed the corpses lined up on the
floor. He would have preferred Mildred in the bathtub.

"Yeah," said the Westerner, edging away from Clive as if he didn't like him.

"The bodies were put into a few of the exhibitions. Like the wax figures. They say that, but they don't show a picture of it," said Clive.

"Yeah," said the Westerner, and went on with his hamburger.

Clive felt let down and somehow insulted. His face grew a little warm as he stared back at his newspapers. In fact, anger was growing very quickly inside him, making his heart go faster, as it did when he passed Madame Thibault's Waxwork Horrors, though now the sensation was not at all pleasant. Clive put on a smile, however, and turned again to the man on his left. "I mention it, because I did it. That's my work there." He pointed at the picture of the corpses.

"Listen, boy," said the Westerner, chewing, "you just keep to yourself tonight. Okay? We ain't botherin' you, and don't you go botherin' us." He laughed a little, and glanced at his companion.

His friend was staring at Clive, but looked away at once when Clive looked at him.

This was a double rebuff, and quite enough for Clive. Clive got his money out and paid for his unfinished food with a dollar bill and a fifty-cent piece. He left the change and walked to the sliding door exit.

"But y'know, maybe that kid ain't kiddin'," Clive heard one of the men say.

Clive turned and said, "*I* ain't kiddin'!" Then he went out into the night.

Clive slept at a YMCA. The next day, he half expected he would be picked up by any passing cop on the beat, but he wasn't, and he passed a few. He got a lift to another town, nearer his home town. The day's newspapers brought no mention of his name, and no clues. In another café that evening almost the identical conversation took place between Clive and a couple of fellows around his own age. They didn't believe him. It was stupid of them, Clive thought, and he wondered if they were pretending? Or lying?

Clive hitched his way to his hometown, and headed for the police station. He was curious to see what *they* would say. He imagined what his mother would say after he confessed. Probably the same thing she had said to her friends sometimes, or that she'd said to a policeman when he was sixteen and had stolen a car:

"Clive hasn't been the same boy since his father went away. I know he needs a man around the house, a man to look up to, imitate, y'know. That's what people tell me. Since fourteen, Clive's been asking me questions like, 'Who am I, anyway?' and 'Am I a person, mom?' " Clive could see and hear her already in the police station.

"I have an important confession to make," Clive said to a guard, or somebody, sitting at a desk at the front of the station.

The guard's attitude was rude and suspicious, Clive thought, but he was told to walk to an office, where he spoke with a police officer who had gray hair and a fat face. Clive told his story.

"Where do you go to school, Clive?"

"I don't. I'm eighteen." Clive told him about his job at Simmons's Grocery.

"Clive, you've got troubles, but they're not the ones you're talking about," said the officer.

Clive had to wait in a room, and nearly an hour later a psychiatrist was brought in. Then his mother. Clive became more and more impatient. They didn't believe him. They were saying he was a typical case of false confessing in order to attract attention to himself. His mother's repeated statements about his asking questions like "Am I a person?" only seemed to corroborate the psychiatrist and the police in their opinion.

Clive was to report somewhere twice a week for psychiatric therapy.

He fumed. He refused to go back to Simmons's Grocery, but found another delivery job, because he liked having a little money in his pocket, and he was fast on his bicycle and honest with the change.

"You haven't *found* the murderer, have you?" Clive said to the psychiatrist, associating him, Clive realized, with the police. "You're all the biggest bunch of jackasses I've ever seen in my life!"

The psychiatrist lost his temper, which was at least human.

"You'll never get anywhere talking to people like that, boy."

Clive said, "Some perfectly ordinary strangers in Indiana said, 'Maybe that kid ain't kiddin'.' They seem to have had more sense than *you!*"

The psychiatrist laughed.

Clive smoldered. One thing might have helped to prove his story, Woodrow Wilson's necktie, which still hung in his closet. But these bastards damned well didn't deserve to see that tie. Even as he ate his suppers with his mother, went to movies with her, and delivered groceries, he was planning. He'd do something more important next time: start a fire in the depths of a big building, plant a bomb somewhere, take a machine gun up to some penthouse and let 'em have it down on the street. Kill a hundred people at least. They'd have to come up in the building to get him. They'd know then. They'd treat him like somebody who existed.

One for the Islands

The voyage wasn't to be much longer.

Most people were bound for the mainland, which was not far at all now. Others were bound for the islands to the west, some of which were very far indeed.

Dan was bound for a certain island that he believed probably farther than any of the others the ship would touch at. He supposed that he would be about the last passenger to disembark.

On the sixth day of the smooth, uneventful voyage, he was in excellent spirits. He enjoyed the company of his fellow-passengers, had joined them a few times in the games that were always in progress on the top deck forward, but mostly he strolled the deck with his pipe in his mouth and a book under his arm, the pipe unlighted and the book forgotten, gazing serenely at the horizon and thinking of the island to which he was going. It would be the finest island of them all, Dan imagined. For some months now, he had devoted much of his time to imagining its terrain. There was no doubt, he decided finally, that he knew more about his island than any man alive, a fact which made him smile whenever he thought of it. No, no one would ever know a hundredth of what he knew about his island, though he had never seen it. But then, perhaps no one else had ever seen it, either.

Dan was happiest when strolling the deck, alone, letting his eyes drift from soft cloud to horizon, from sun to sea, thinking always that his island might come into view before the mainland. He would know its outline at once, he was sure of that. Strangely, it would be like a place he had always known, but secretly, telling no one. And there he would finally be alone.

It startled him sometimes, unpleasantly, too, suddenly to encounter, face to face, a passenger coming round a corner. He found it disturbing to bump into a hurrying steward in one of the twisting, turning corridors of D-deck, which being third class was more like a catacomb than the rest, and which was the deck where Dan had his cabin. Then there had been the time, the second day of the voyage, when for an instant he saw very close to his eyes the

ridged floor of the corridor, with a cigarette butt between two
ridges, a chewing-gum wrapper, and a few discarded matches. That
had been unpleasant, too.

"Are you for the mainland?" asked Mrs. Gibson-Leyden, one
of the first-class passengers, as they stood at the rail one evening.

Dan smiled a little and shook his head. "No, the islands," he
said pleasantly, rather surprised that Mrs. Gibson-Leyden didn't
know by now. But on the other hand, there had been little talk
among the passengers as to where each was going. "You're for the
mainland, I take it?" He spoke to be friendly knowing quite well
that Mrs. Gibson-Leyden was for the mainland.

"Oh, yes," Mrs. Gibson-Leyden said. "My husband had some
idea of going to an island, but I said, not for me!"

She laughed with an air of satisfaction, and Dan nodded. He
liked Mrs. Gibson-Leyden because she was cheerful. It was more
than could be said for most of the first-class passengers. Now he
leaned his forearms on the rail and looked out at the wake of
moonlight on the sea that shimmered like the back of a gigantic
sea dragon with silver scales. Dan couldn't imagine that anyone
would go to the mainland when there were islands in abundance,
but then he had never been able to understand such things, and
with a person like Mrs. Gibson-Leyden, there was no use in trying to discuss them and to understand. Dan drew gently on his
empty pipe. He could smell a fragrance of lavender cologne from
Mrs. Gibson-Leyden's direction. It reminded him of a girl he had
once known, and he was amused now that he could feel drawn to
Mrs. Gibson-Leyden, certainly old enough to have been his
mother, because she wore a familiar scent.

"Well, I'm supposed to meet my husband back in the game
room," Mrs. Gibson-Leyden said, moving away. "He went down to
get a sweater."

Dan nodded, awkwardly now. Her departure made him feel
abandoned, absurdly lonely, and immediately he reproached himself for not having made more of an effort at communication with

her. He smiled, straightened, and peered into the darkness over his left shoulder, where the mainland would appear before dawn, then his island, later.

Two people, a man and a woman, walked slowly down the deck, side by side, their figures quite black in the darkness. Dan was conscious of their separateness from each other. Another isolated figure, short and fat, moved into the light of the windows in the superstructure: Dr. Eubanks, Dan recognized. Forward, Dan saw a group of people standing on deck and at the rails, all isolated, too. He had a vision of stewards and stewardesses below, eating their solitary meals at tiny tables in the corridors, hurrying about with towels, trays, menus. They were all alone, too. There was nobody who touched anybody, he thought, no man who held his wife's hand, no lovers whose lips met—at least he hadn't seen any so far on this voyage.

Dan straightened still taller. An overwhelming sense of alone-ness, of his own isolation, had taken possession of him, and because his impulse was to shrink within himself, he unconsciously stood as tall as he could. But he could not look at the ship any longer, and turned back to the sea.

It seemed to him that only the moon spread its arms, laid its web protectively, lovingly, over the sea's body. He stared at the veils of moonlight as hard as he could, for as long as he could—which was perhaps twenty-five seconds—then went below to his cabin and to sleep.

He was awakened by the sound of running feet on the deck, and a murmur of excited voices.

The mainland, he thought at once, and threw off his bedcov-ers. He did want a good look at the mainland. Then as his head cleared of sleep, he realized that the excitement on deck must be about something else. There was more running now, a woman's wondering "Oh!" that was half a scream, half an exclamation of pleasure. Dan hurried into his clothes and ran out of his cabin.

His view from the A-deck companionway made him stop and

draw in his breath. The ship was sailing *downward,* had been sailing downward on a long, broad path in the sea itself. Dan had never seen anything like it. No one else had either, apparently. No wonder everyone was so excited.

"When?" asked a man who was running after the hurrying captain. "Did you see it? What happened?"

The captain had no time to answer him.

"It's all right. This is right," said a petty officer, whose calm, serious face contrasted strangely with the wide-eyed alertness of everyone else.

"One doesn't notice it below," Dan said quickly to Mr. Steyne who was standing near him, and felt idiotic at once, because what did it matter whether one felt it below or not? The ship was sailing downward, the sea sloped downward at about a twenty degree angle with the horizon, and such a thing had never been heard of before, even in the Bible.

Dan ran to join the passengers who were crowding the forward deck. "When did it start? I mean, where?" Dan asked the person nearest him.

The person shrugged, though his face was as excited, as anxious as the rest.

Dan strained to see what the water looked like at the side of the swath, for the slope did not seem more than two miles broad. But whatever was happening, whether the swath ended in a sharp edge or sloped up to the main body of the sea, he could not make out, because a fine mist obscured the sea on either side. Now he noticed the golden light that lay on everything around them, the swath, the atmosphere, the horizon before them. The light was no stronger on one side than on the other, so it could not have been the sun. Dan couldn't find the sun, in fact. But the rest of the sky and the higher body of the sea behind them was bright as morning.

"Has anybody seen the mainland?" Dan asked, interrupting the babble around him.

"No," said a man.

"There's no mainland," said the same unruffled petty officer.

Dan had a sudden feeling of having been duped.

"This is right," the petty officer added laconically. He was winding a thin line around and round his arm, bracing it on palm and elbow.

"Right?" asked Dan.

"This is it," said the petty officer.

"That's right, this is it," a man at the rail confirmed, speaking over his shoulder.

"No islands, either?" asked Dan, alarmed.

"No," said the petty officer, not unkindly, but in an abrupt way that hurt Dan in his breast.

"Well—what's all this talk about the mainland?" Dan asked.

"Talk," said the petty officer, with a twinkle now.

"Isn't it won-derful!" said a woman's voice behind him, and Dan turned to see Mrs. Gibson-Leyden—Mrs. Gibson-Leyden who had been so eager for the mainland—gazing rapturously at the empty white and gold mist.

"Do you know about this? How much farther does it go?" asked Dan, but the petty officer was gone. Dan wished he could be as calm as everyone else—generally he was calmer—but how could he be calm about his vanished island? How could the rest just stand there at the rails, for the most part taking it all quite calmly, he could tell by the voices now and their casual postures.

Dan saw the petty officer again and ran after him. "What happens?" he asked. "What happens next?" His questions struck him as foolish, but they were as good as any.

"This is *it,*" said the petty officer with a smile. "Good God, boy!"

Dan bit his lips.

"This is *it!*" repeated the petty officer. "What did you expect?"

Dan hesitated. "Land," he said in a voice that made it almost a question.

The petty officer laughed silently and shook his head. "You can get off any time you like."

Dan gave a startled look around him. It was true, people were getting off at the port rail, stepping over the side with their suitcases. "Onto what?" Dan asked, aghast.

The petty officer laughed again, and disdaining to answer him, walked slowly away with his coiled line.

Dan caught his arm. "Get off here? Why?"

"As good a place as any. Whatever spot strikes your fancy." The petty officer chuckled. "It's all alike."

"All sea?"

"There's no sea," said the petty officer. "But there's certainly no land."

And there went Mr. and Mrs. Gibson-Leyden now, off the starboard rail.

"Hey!" Dan called to them, but they didn't turn.

Dan watched them disappear quickly. He blinked his eyes. They had not been holding hands, but they had been near each other, they had been together.

Suddenly Dan realized that if he got off the boat as they had done, he could still be alone, if he wanted to be. It was strange, of course, to think of stepping out into space. But the instant he was able to conceive it, barely conceive it, it became right to do it. He could feel it filling him with a gradual but overpowering certainty, that he only reluctantly yielded to. This was right, as the petty officer had said. And this was as good a place as any.

Dan looked around him. The boat was really almost empty now. He might as well be last, he thought. He'd meant to be last. He'd go down and get his suitcase packed. What a nuisance! The mainland passengers, of course, had been packed since the afternoon before.

Dan turned impatiently on the companionway where he had once nearly fallen, and he climbed up again. He didn't want his suitcase after all. He didn't want anything with him.

He put a foot up on the starboard rail and stepped off. He walked several yards on an invisible ground that was softer than grass. It wasn't what he had thought it would be like, yet now that he was here, it wasn't strange, either. In fact there was even that sense of recognition that he had imagined he would feel when he set foot on his island. He turned for a last look at the ship that was still on its downward course. Then suddenly, he was impatient with himself. Why look at a ship, he asked himself, and abruptly turned and went on.

A Curious Suicide

Dr. Stephen McCullough had a first-class compartment to himself on the express from Paris to Geneva. He sat browsing in one of the medical quarterlies he had brought from America, but he was not concentrating. He was toying with the idea of murder. That was why he had taken the train instead of flying, to give himself time to think or perhaps merely dream.

He was a serious man of forty-five, a little overweight, with a prominent and spreading nose, a brown mustache, brown-rimmed glasses, a receding hairline. His eyebrows were tense with an inward anxiety, which his patients often thought a concern with their problems. Actually, he was unhappily married, and though he refused to quarrel with Lillian—that meant answer her back—there was discord between them. In Paris yesterday he had answered Lillian back, and on a ridiculous matter about whether he or she would take back to a shop on the Rue Royale an evening bag that Lillian had decided she did not want. He had been angry not because he had had to return the bag, but because he had agreed, in a weak moment fifteen minutes before, to visit Roger Fane in Geneva.

"Go and see him, Steve," Lillian had said yesterday morning. "You're so close to Geneva now, why not? Think of the pleasure it'd give Roger."

What pleasure? Why? But Dr. McCullough had rung Roger at the American Embassy in Geneva, and Roger had been very friendly, much too friendly, of course, and had said that he must come and stay a few days and that he had plenty of room to put him up. Dr. McCullough had agreed to spend one night. Then he was going to fly to Rome to join Lillian.

Dr. McCullough detested Roger Fane. It was the kind of hatred that time does nothing to diminish. Roger Fane, seventeen years ago, had married the woman Dr. McCullough loved. Margaret. Margaret had died a year ago in an automobile accident on an Alpine road. Roger Fane was smug, cautious, mightily pleased with himself and not very intelligent. Seventeen years ago, Roger

Fane had told Margaret that he, Stephen McCullough, was having a secret affair with another girl. Nothing was further from
the truth, but before Stephen could prove anything, Margaret
had married Roger. Dr. McCullough had not expected the marriage to last, but it had, and finally Dr. McCullough had married
Lillian whose face resembled Margaret's a little, but that was the
only similarity. In the past seventeen years, Dr. McCullough
had seen Roger and Margaret perhaps three times when they had
come to New York on short trips. He had not seen Roger since
Margaret's death.

Now as the train shot through the French countryside, Dr.
McCullough reflected on the satisfaction that murdering Roger
Fane might give him. He had never before thought of murdering
anybody, but yesterday evening while he was taking a bath in
the Paris hotel, after the telephone conversation with Roger, a
thought had come to him in regard to murder: most murderers
were caught because they left some clue, despite their efforts to
erase all the clues. Many murderers wanted to be caught, the doctor realized, and unconsciously planted a clue that led the police
straight to them. In the Leopold and Loeb case, one of them had
dropped his glasses at the scene, for instance. But suppose a murderer deliberately left a dozen clues, practically down to his calling
card? It seemed to Dr. McCullough that the very obviousness of
it would throw suspicion off. Especially if the person were a man
like himself, well thought of, a nonviolent type. Also, there'd be
no motive that anyone could see, because Dr. McCullough had
never even told Lillian that he had loved the woman Roger Fane
had married. Of course, a few of his old friends knew it, but
Dr. McCullough hadn't mentioned Margaret or Roger Fane in
a decade.

He imagined Roger's apartment formal and gloomy, perhaps
with a servant prowling about full time, a servant who slept in. A
servant would complicate things. Let's say there wasn't a servant
who slept in, that he and Roger would be having a nightcap in the

living room or in Roger's study, and then just before saying good night, Dr. McCullough would pick up a heavy paperweight or a big vase and—Then he would calmly take his leave. Of course, the bed should be slept in, since he was supposed to stay the night, so perhaps the morning would be better for the crime than the evening. The essential thing was to leave quietly and at the time he was supposed to leave. But the doctor found himself unable to plot in much detail after all.

Roger Fane's street in Geneva looked just as Dr. McCullough had imagined it—a narrow, curving street that combined business establishments with old private dwellings—and it was not too well lighted when Dr. McCullough's taxi entered it at 9 P.M., yet in law-abiding Switzerland, the doctor supposed, dark streets held few dangers for anyone. The front door buzzed in response to his ring, and Dr. McCullough opened it. The door was heavy as a bank vault's door.

"Hullo!" Roger's voice called cheerily down the stairwell. "Come up! I'm on the third floor. Fourth to you, I suppose."

"Be right there!" Dr. McCullough said, shy about raising his voice in the presence of the closed doors on either side of the hall. He had telephoned Roger a few moments ago from the railway station, because Roger had said he would meet him. Roger had apologized and said he had been held up at a meeting at his office, and would Steve mind hopping a taxi and coming right over? Dr. McCullough suspected that Roger had not been held up at all, but simply hadn't wanted to show him the courtesy of being at the station.

"Well, well, Steve!" said Roger, pumping Dr. McCullough's hand. "It's great to see you again. Come in, come in. Is that thing heavy?" Roger made a pass at the doctor's suitcase, but the doctor caught it up first.

"Not at all. Good to see you again, Roger." He went into the apartment.

There were oriental rugs, ornate lamps that gave off dim light.

It was even stuffier than Dr. McCullough had anticipated. Roger looked a trifle thinner. He was shorter than the doctor, and had sparse blond hair. His weak face perpetually smiled. Both had eaten dinner, so they drank scotch in the living room.

"So you're joining Lillian in Rome tomorrow," said Roger. "Sorry you won't be staying longer. I'd intended to drive you out to the country tomorrow evening to meet a friend of mine. A woman," Roger added with a smile.

"Oh? Too bad. Yes, I'll be off on the one o'clock plane tomorrow afternoon. I made the reservation from Paris." Dr. McCullough found himself speaking automatically. Strangely, he felt a little drunk, though he'd taken only a couple of sips of his scotch. It was because of the falsity of the situation, he thought, the falsity of his being here at all, of his pretending friendship or at least friendliness. Roger's smile irked him, so merry and yet so forced. Roger hadn't referred to Margaret, though Dr. McCullough had not seen him since she died. But then, neither had the doctor referred to her, even to give a word of condolence. And already, it seemed, Roger had another female interest. Roger was just over forty, still trim of figure and bright of eye. And Margaret, that jewel among women, was just something that had come his way, stayed a while, and departed, Dr. McCullough supposed. Roger looked not at all bereaved.

The doctor detested Roger fully as much as he had on the train, but the reality of Roger Fane was somewhat dismaying. If he killed him, he would have to touch him, feel the resistance of his flesh at any rate with the object he hit him with. And what was the servant situation? As if Roger read his mind, he said:

"I've a girl who comes in to clean every morning at ten and leaves at twelve. If you want her to do anything for you, wash and iron a shirt or something like that, don't hesitate. She's very fast, or can be' if you ask her. Her name's Yvonne."

Then the telephone rang. Roger spoke in French. His face fell slightly as he agreed to do something that the other person was asking him to do. Roger said to the doctor:

"Of all irritating things. I've got to catch the seven o'clock plane to Zurich tomorrow. Some visiting fireman's being welcomed at a breakfast. So, old man, I suppose I'll be gone before you're out of bed."

"Oh!" Dr. McCullough found himself chuckling. "You think doctors aren't used to early calls? Of course I'll get up to tell you good-bye—see you off."

Roger's smile widened slightly. "Well, we'll see. I certainly won't wake you for it. Make yourself at home and I'll leave a note for Yvonne to prepare coffee and rolls. Or would you like a more substantial brunch around eleven?"

Dr. McCullough was not thinking about what Roger was saying. He had just noticed a rectangular marble pen and pencil holder on the desk where the telephone stood. He was looking at Roger's high and faintly pink forehead. "Oh, brunch," said the doctor vaguely. "No, no, for goodness' sake. They feed you enough on the plane." And then his thoughts leapt to Lillian and the quarrel yesterday in Paris. Hostility smoldered in him. Had Roger ever quarreled with Margaret? Dr. McCullough could not imagine Margaret being unfair, being mean. It was no wonder Roger's face looked relaxed and untroubled.

"A penny for your thoughts," said Roger, getting up to replenish his glass.

The doctor's glass was still half full.

"I suppose I'm a bit tired," said Dr. McCullough, and passed his hand across his forehead. When he lifted his head again, he saw a photograph of Margaret which he had not noticed before on the top of the highboy on his right. Margaret in her twenties, as she had looked when Roger married her, as she had looked when the doctor had so loved her. Dr. McCullough looked suddenly at Roger. His hatred returned in a wave that left him physically

weak. "I suppose I'd better turn in," he said, setting his glass carefully on the little table in front of him, standing up. Roger had
showed him his bedroom.

"Sure you wouldn't like a spot of brandy?" asked Roger. "You
look all in." Roger smiled cockily, standing very straight.

The tide of the doctor's anger flowed back. He picked up the
marble slab with one hand, and before Roger could step back,
smashed him in the forehead with its base. It was a blow that
would kill, the doctor knew. Roger fell and without even a last
twitch lay still and limp. The doctor set the marble back where it
had been, picked up the pen and pencil which had fallen, and
replaced them in their holders, then wiped the marble with his
handkerchief where his fingers had touched it and also the pen
and pencil. Roger's forehead was bleeding slightly. He felt Roger's
still-warm wrist and found no pulse. Then he went out the door
and down the hall to his own room.

He awakened the next morning at 8:15, after a not very sound
night's sleep. He showered in the bathroom between his room and
Roger's bedroom, shaved, dressed and left the house at a quarter
past nine. A hall went from his room past the kitchen to the flat's
door; it had not been necessary to cross the living room, and even
if he had glanced into the living room through the door he had
not closed, Roger's body would have been out of sight to him. Dr.
McCullough had not glanced in.

At 5:30 P.M. he was in Rome, riding in a taxi from the airport
to the Hotel Majestic where Lillian awaited him. Lillian was out,
however. The doctor had some coffee sent up, and it was then that
he noticed his briefcase was missing. He had wanted to lie on the
bed and drink coffee and read his medical quarterlies. Now he
remembered distinctly: he had for some reason carried his briefcase into the living room last evening. This did not disturb him at
all. It was exactly what he should have done on purpose if he had
thought of it. His name and his New York address were written in
the slot of the briefcase. And Dr. McCullough supposed that

Roger had written his name in full in some engagement book along with the time of his arrival.

He found Lillian in good humor. She had bought a lot of things in the Via Condotti. They had dinner and then took a carozza ride through the Villa Borghese, to the Piazza di Spagna and the Piazza del Populo. If there were anything in the papers about Roger, Dr. McCullough was ignorant of it. He bought only the Paris *Herald-Tribune,* which was a morning paper.

The news came the next morning as he and Lillian were breakfasting at Donay's in the Via Veneto. It was in the Paris *Herald-Tribune,* and there was a picture of Roger Fane on the front page, a serious official picture of him in a wing collar.

"Good Lord!" said Lillian. "Why—it happened the night you were there!"

Looking over her shoulder, Dr. McCullough pretended surprise. " '—died some time between eight P.M. and three A.M.,' " the doctor read. "I said good night to him about eleven, I think. Went into my room."

"You didn't *hear* anything?"

"No. My room was down a hall. I closed my door."

"And the next morning. You didn't—"

"I told you, Roger had to catch a seven o'clock plane. I assumed he was gone. I left the house around nine."

"And all the time he was in the living room!" Lillian said with a gasp. "Steve! Why, this is terrible!"

Was it, Dr. McCullough wondered. Was it so terrible for her? Her voice did not sound really concerned. He looked into her wide eyes. "It's certainly terrible—but I'm not responsible, God knows. Don't worry, Lillian."

The police were at the Hotel Majestic when they returned, waiting for Dr. McCullough in the lobby. They were both plain-clothes Swiss police, and they spoke English. They interviewed Dr. McCullough at a table in a corner of the lobby. Lillian had, at Dr. McCullough's insistence, gone up to their room. Dr. McCullough had wondered why the police had not come for him hours earlier than this—it was so simple to check the passenger list of planes leaving Geneva—but he soon found out why. The maid Yvonne had not come to clean yesterday morning, so Roger Fane's body had not been discovered until 6 P.M. yesterday, when his office had become alarmed by his absence and sent someone around to his apartment to investigate.

"This is your briefcase, I think," said the slender blond officer with a smile, opening a large manila envelope he had been carrying under his arm.

"Yes, thank you very much. I realized today that I'd left it." The doctor took it and laid it on his lap.

The two Swiss watched him quietly.

"This is very shocking," Dr. McCullough said. "It's hard for me to realize." He was impatient for them to make their charge—if they were going to—and ask him to return to Geneva with them. They both seemed almost in awe of him.

"How well did you know Mr. Fane?" asked the other officer.

"Not too well. I've known him many years, but we were never close friends. I hadn't seen him in five years, I think." Dr. McCullough spoke steadily and in his usual tone.

"Mr. Fane was still fully dressed, so he had not gone to bed. You are sure you heard no disturbance that night?"

"I did not," the doctor answered for the second time. A silence. "Have you any clues as to who might have done it?"

"Oh, yes, yes," the blond man said matter of factly. "We suspect the brother of the maid Yvonne. He was drunk that night and hasn't an alibi for the time of the crime. He and his sister live together and that night he went off with his sister's batch of keys—among which were the keys to Mr. Fane's apartment. He didn't come back until nearly noon yesterday. Yvonne was worried about him, which is why she didn't go to Mr. Fane's apartment yesterday—that plus the fact she couldn't have got in. She tried to telephone at eight-thirty yesterday morning to say she wouldn't be coming, but she got no answer. We've questioned the brother Anton. He's a ne'er-do-well." The man shrugged.

Dr. McCullough remembered hearing the telephone ring at eight-thirty. "But—what was the motive?"

"Oh—resentment. Robbery maybe if he'd been sober enough to find anything to take. He's a case for a psychiatrist or an alcoholic ward. Mr. Fane knew him, so he might have let him into the apartment, or he could have walked in, since he had the keys. Yvonne said that Mr. Fane had been trying for months to get her to live apart from her brother. Her brother beats her and takes her money. Mr. Fane had spoken to the brother a couple of times, and it's on our record that Mr. Fane once had to call the police to get Anton out of the apartment when he came there looking for his sister. That incident happened at nine in the evening, an hour when his sister is never there. You see how off his head he is."

Dr. McCullough cleared his throat and asked, "Has Anton confessed to it?"

"Oh, the same as. Poor chap, I really don't think he knows what he's doing half the time. But at least in Switzerland there's no capital punishment. He'll have enough time to dry out in jail, all right." He glanced at his colleague and they both stood up. "Thank you very much, Dr. McCullough."

"You're very welcome," said the doctor. "Thank you for the briefcase."

Dr. McCullough went upstairs with his briefcase to his room. "What did they say?" Lillian asked as he came in.

"They think the brother of the maid did it," said Dr. McCullough. "Fellow who's an alcoholic and who seems to have had it in for Roger. Some ne'er-do-well." Frowning, he went into the bathroom to wash his hands. He suddenly detested himself, detested Lillian's long sigh, an "Ah–h" of relief and joy.

"Thank God, thank God!" Lillian said. "Do you know what

this would have meant if they'd—if they'd have accused *you*?" she asked in a softer voice, as if the walls had ears, and she came closer to the bathroom door.

"Certainly," Dr. McCullough said, and felt a burst of anger in his blood. "I'd have had a hell of a time proving I was innocent, since I was right there at the time."

"Exactly. You couldn't have proved you were innocent. Thank God for this Anton, whoever he is." Her small face glowed, her eyes twinkled. "A ne'er-do-well. Ha! He did us some good!" She laughed shrilly and turned on one heel.

"I don't see why you have to gloat," he said, drying his hands carefully. "It's a sad story."

"Sadder than if they'd blamed you? Don't be so—so altruistic, dear. Or rather, think of us. Husband kills old rival-in-love after— let's see—seventeen years, isn't it? And after eleven years of marriage to another woman. The torch still burns high. Do you think I'd like that?"

"Lillian, what're you talking about?" He came out of the bathroom scowling.

"You know exactly. You think I don't know you were in love with Margaret? *Still* are? You think I don't know you killed Roger?" Her gray eyes looked at him with a wild challenge. Her head was tipped to one side, her hands on her hips.

He felt tongue-tied, paralyzed. They stared at each other for perhaps fifteen seconds, while his mind moved tentatively over the abyss her words had just spread before him. He hadn't known that she still thought of Margaret. Of course she'd known about Margaret. But who had kept the story alive in her mind? Perhaps himself by his silence, the doctor realized. But the future was what mattered. Now she had something to hold over his head, something by which she could control him forever. "My dear, you are mistaken."

But Lillian with a toss of her head turned and walked away, and the doctor knew he had not won.

Absolutely nothing was said about the matter for the rest of the day. They lunched, spent a leisurely hour in the Vatican museum, but Dr. McCullough's mind was on other things than Michelangelo's paintings. He was going to go to Geneva and confess the thing, not for decency's sake or because his conscience bothered him, but because Lillian's attitude was insupportable. It was less supportable than a stretch in prison. He managed to get away long enough to make a telephone call at five P.M. There was a plane to Geneva at 7:20 P.M. At 6:15 P.M., he left their hotel room empty-handed and took a taxi to Ciampino airport. He had his passport and traveler's checks.

He arrived in Geneva before eleven that evening, and called the police. At first, they were not willing to tell him the whereabouts of the man accused of murdering Roger Fane, but Dr. McCullough gave his name and said he had some important information, and then the Swiss police told him where Anton Carpeau was being held. Dr. McCullough took a taxi to what seemed the outskirts of Geneva. It was a new white building, not at all like a prison.

Here he was greeted by one of the plainclothes officers who had come to see him, the blond one. "Dr. McCullough," he said with a faint smile. "You have some information, you say? I am afraid it is a little late."

"Oh?—Why?"

"Anton Carpeau has just killed himself—by bashing his head against the wall of his cell. Just twenty minutes ago." The man gave a hopeless shrug.

"Good God," Dr. McCullough said softly.

"But what was your information?"

The doctor hesitated. The words wouldn't come. And then he realized that it was cowardice and shame that kept him silent. He had never felt so worthless in his life, and he felt infinitely lower than the drunken ne'er-do-well who had killed himself. "I'd rather not. In this case—I mean—it's so all over, isn't it? It was something else against Anton, I thought—and what's the use now? It's bad enough—" The words stopped.

"Yes, I suppose so," said the Swiss.

"So—I'll say good night."

"Good night, Dr. McCullough."

Then the doctor walked on into the night, aimlessly. He felt a curious emptiness, a nothingness in himself that was not like any mood he had ever known. His plan for murder had succeeded, but it had dragged worse tragedies in its wake. Anton Carpeau. And *Lillian*. In a strange way, he had killed himself just as much as he had killed Roger Fane. He was now a dead man, a walking dead man.

Half an hour later, he stood on a formal bridge looking down at the black water of Lake Leman. He stared down a long while, and imagined his body toppling over and over, striking the water with not much of a splash, sinking. He stared hard at the blackness that looked so solid but would be so yielding, so willing to swallow him into death. But he hadn't even the courage or the despair as yet for suicide. One day, however, he would, he knew. One day when the planes of cowardice and courage met at the proper angle. And that day would be a surprise to him and to everyone else who knew him. Then his hands that gripped the stone parapet pushed him back, and the doctor walked on heavily. He would see about a hotel for tonight, and then tomorrow arrange to get back to Rome.

The Baby Spoon

Claude Lamm, Professor of English Literature and Poetry, had been on the faculty of Columbia University for ten years. Short and inclined to plumpness, with a bald spot in the middle of his close-cropped black hair, he did not look like a college professor, but rather like a small businessman hiding for some reason in the clothes he thought a college professor should wear—good tweed jackets with leather patches on the elbows, unpressed gray flannels and unshined shoes of any sort. He lived in one of the great dreary apartment buildings that clump east and south of Columbia University, a gloomy, ash-colored building with a shaky elevator and an ugly miscellany of smells old and new inside it. Claude Lamm rendered his sunless, five-room apartment still more somber by cramming it with sodden-looking sofas, with books and periodicals and photographs of classic edifices and landscapes about which he professed to be sentimental but actually was not.

Seven years ago he had married Margaret Cullen, one of those humdrum, colorless individuals who look as if they might be from anywhere except New York and turn out, incredibly, to be native New Yorkers. She was fifty, eight years older than Claude, with a plain, open countenance and an air of desperate inferiority. Claude had met her through another professor who knew Margaret's father, and had married her because of certain unconscious drives in himself towards the maternal. But under Margaret's matronly exterior lay a nature that was half childish, too, and peculiarly irritating to Claude. Apart from her cooking and sewing—she did neither well—and the uninspired routine that might be called the running of the house, she had no interests. Except for an occasional exchange of letters, which she bored Claude by reading aloud at the table, she had detached herself from her old friends.

Claude came home about five most afternoons, had some tea and planned his work and reading for the evening. At 6:15, he drank a martini without ice and read the evening paper in the living room, while Margaret prepared their early dinner. They dined on shoulder lamb chops or meat loaf, often on cheese and macaroni, which Margaret was fond of, and Margaret stirred her coffee with the silver baby spoon she had used the first evening Claude had met her, holding the spoon by the tip end of the handle in order to reach the bottom of the cup. After dinner, Claude retired to his study—a book-glutted cubicle with an old black leather couch in it, although he did not sleep here—to read and correct papers and to browse in his bookshelves for anything that piqued his aimless curiosity.

Every two weeks or so, he asked Professor Millikin, a Shake-speare scholar, or Assistant Professor George and his wife to come to dinner. Three or four times a year, the apartment was thrown open to about twelve students from his special readings classes, who came and ate Dundee cake and drank tea. Margaret would sit on a cushion on the floor, because there were never enough chairs, and of course one young man after another would offer his chair to her. "Oh, no, thank you!" Margaret would protest with a lisping coyness quite unlike her usual manner, "I'm perfectly comfortable here. Sitting on the floor makes me feel like a little girl again." She would look up at the young men as if she expected them to tell her she looked like a little girl, too, which to Claude's disgust the young men sometimes did. The little girl mood always came over Margaret in the company of men, and always made Claude sneer when he saw it. Claude sneered easily and uncontrollably, hiding it unconsciously in the act of putting his cigarette holder between his teeth, or rubbing the side of his nose with a forefinger. Claude had keen, suspicious brown eyes. No feature of his face was remarkable, but it was not a face one forgot either. It was the rest-lessness, the furtiveness in his face that one noticed first and remembered. At the teas, Margaret would use her baby spoon, too, which as likely as not would start a conversation. Then Claude would move out of hearing.

Claude did not like the way the young men looked at his wife—disappointedly, a little pityingly, always solemnly. Claude was ashamed of her before them. She should have been beautiful and gay, a nymph of the soul, a fair face that would accord with the love poems of Donne and Sidney. Well, she wasn't.

Claude's marriage to Margaret might have been comparable to a marriage to his housekeeper, if not for emotional entanglements that made him passionately hate her as well as passionately need her. He hated her childishness with a vicious, personal resentment. He hated almost as much her competent, maternal ministerings to him, her taking his clothes to the cleaners, for instance; which was all he tolerated her for, he knew, and why he had her now instead of his nymph. When he had been down with flu one winter and Margaret had waited on him hand and foot, he had sneered often at her retreating back, hating her, really hating her obsequious devotion to him. Claude had despised his mother and she, too, between periods of neglect and erratic ill-temper, had been capable of smothering affection and attention. But the nearest he came to expressing his hatred was when he announced casually, once a week or oftener:

"Winston's coming over for a while tonight."

"Oh," Margaret would reply with a tremor in her voice. "Well, I suppose he'd like some of the raisin cake later. Or maybe a sandwich of the meat loaf."

Winston loved to eat at Claude's house. Or rather, he was always hungry. Winston was a genuinely starving poet who lived in a genuine garret at the top of a brownstone house in the West Seventies. He had been a student of Claude's three years ago, a highly promising student whose brilliant, aggressive mind had so dominated his classmates that the classes had been hardly more than conversations between Claude and Winston. Claude was immensely fond of Winston and flattered by Winston's fondness for him. From the first, it had excited Claude in a strange and pleasant way to catch Winston's smile, Winston's wink even, the glint of mad humor in his eyes, in the midst of Winston's flurry of words in class. While at Columbia, Winston had published several poems in poetry magazines and literary magazines. He had written a poem called "The Booming Bittern," a mournful satire on an undergraduate's life and directionless rebellion, that Claude had thought might take the place in Winston's career that "Prufrock" had taken in Eliot's. The poem had been published in some quarterly but had attracted no important attention.

Claude had expected Winston to go far and do him credit. Winston had published only one small book of verse since leaving college. Something had happened to Winston's easy, original flow of thought. Something had happened to his self-confidence after leaving college, as if the wells of inspiration were drying up along with the sap and vitality of his twenty-four-year-old body. Winston was thin as a rail now. He had always been thin, but now he slouched, hung his head like a wronged and resentful man, and his eyes under the hard, straight brows looked anxious, hostile and unhappy. He clung to Claude with the persistence of a maltreated child clinging to the one human being who had ever given him kindness and encouragement. Winston was working now on a novel in the form of a long poem. He had submitted part of it to his publishers a year ago, and they had refused to give him an advance. But Claude liked it, and Winston's attitude was, the rest of the world be damned. Claude was keenly aware of Winston's emotional dependence upon him, and managed to hide his own dependence upon Winston in a superior, patronizing manner that he assumed with Winston. Claude's hostility to Margaret found some further release in the contempt that Winston openly showed for her intellect.

One evening, more than usually late in arriving, Winston slouched into the living room without a reply to Claude's greeting. He was a head and a half taller than Claude, even stooped, his dark brown hair untidy with wind and rain, his overcoat clutched about his splinter of a body by the hands that were rammed into his pockets. Slowly and without a glance at Margaret, Winston walked across the living room towards Claude's study.

Claude was a little annoyed. This was a mood he didn't know.

"Listen, old man, can you lend me some money?" Winston asked when they were alone in the study, then went on over Claude's surprised murmur, "You've no idea what it took for me to come here and ask you, but now it's done, anyway." He sighed heavily.

Claude had a sudden feeling it hadn't taken anything, and that the despondent mood was only playacting. "You know I've always let you have money if you needed it, Winston. Don't take it so seriously. Sit down." Claude sat down.

Winston did not move. His eyes had their usual fierceness, yet there was an impatient pleading in them, too, like the eyes of a child demanding something rightfully his own. "I mean a lot of money. Five hundred dollars. I need it to work on. Five hundred will see me through six weeks, and I can finish my book without any more interruptions."

Claude winced a little. He'd never see the money again if he lent it to Winston. Winston owed him about two hundred now. It occurred to Claude that Winston had not been so intense about anything since his university days. And it also came to him, swiftly and tragically, that Winston would never finish his book. Winston would always be stuck at the anxious, furious pitch he was now, which was contingent upon his not finishing the book.

"You've got to help me out this last time, Claude," Winston said in a begging tone.

"Let me think it over. I'll write you a note about it tomorrow. How's that, fellow?"

Claude got up and went to his desk for a cigarette. Suddenly he hated Winston for standing there begging for money. Like anybody else, Claude thought bitterly. His lip lifted as he set the cigarette holder between his teeth, and Winston saw it, he knew. Winston never missed anything. Why couldn't tonight have been like all the other evenings, Claude thought, Winston smoking his cigarettes, propping his feet on the corner of his desk, Winston laughing and making him laugh, Winston adoring him for all the jibes he threw at the teaching profession?

"You crumb," Winston's voice said steadily. "You fat, smug sonovabitch of a college professor. You stultifier and castrator of the intellect."

Claude stood where he was, half turned away from Winston. The words might have been a blunt ramrod that Winston had thrust through his skull and down to his feet. Winston had never spoken to him like that, and Claude literally did not know how to take it. Claude was not used to reacting to Winston as he reacted to other people. "I'll write you a note about it tomorrow. I'll just have to figure out how and when," he said shortly, with the dignity of a professor whose position, though not handsomely paid, commanded a certain respect.

"I'm sorry," Winston said, hanging his head.

"Winston, what's the matter with you?"

"I don't know." Winston covered his face with his hands.

Claude felt a swift sense of regret, of disappointment at Winston's weakness. He mustn't let Margaret know, he thought. "Sit down."

Winston sat down. He sipped the little glass of whiskey Claude poured from the bottle in his desk as if it were a medicine he desperately needed. Then he sprawled his scarecrow legs out in front of him and said something about a book Claude had lent him the last time he was here, a book of poetry criticism. Claude was grateful for the change of subject. Winston talked with his eyes sleepily half-shut, jerking his big head now and then for emphasis, but Claude could see the glint of interest, of affection, of some indefinable speculation about himself through the half closed lids, and could feel the focus of Winston's intense and personal interest like the life-bringing rays of a sun.

Later, they had coffee and sandwiches and cake in the living room with Margaret. Winston grew very animated and entertained

them with a story of his quest for a hotel room in the town of
Jalapa in Mexico, a story pulled like an unexpected toy from the
hotchpotch of Winston's mind, and by Winston's words set in
motion and given a life of its own. Claude felt proud of Winston.
"See what I amuse myself with behind the door of my study, while
you creep about in the dull prison of your own mind," Claude
might have been saying aloud as he glanced at Margaret to see if
she were appreciating Winston.

Claude did not write to Winston the next day. Claude felt he
was in no more need of money than usual, and that Winston's cri-
sis would pass if he and Winston didn't communicate for a while.
Then on the second evening, Margaret told Claude that she had
lost her baby spoon. She had looked the house over for it, she said.

"Maybe it fell behind the refrigerator," Claude suggested.

"I was hoping you'd help me move it."

A smile pulled at Claude's mouth as he seesawed the refrigerator away from the wall. He hoped she had lost the spoon. It was
a silly thing to treasure at the age of fifty, sillier than her high
school scrapbooks and the gilt baby shoe that had sat on her
father's desk and that Margaret had so unbecomingly claimed after
his death. Claude hoped she had swept the spoon into the garbage
by accident and that it was out of the house forever.

"Nothing but dust," Claude said, looking down at the mess of
fine, sticky gray dust on the floor and the refrigerator wires.

The refrigerator was only the beginning. Claude's cooperation
inspired Margaret. That evening she turned the kitchen inside out,
looked behind all the furniture in the living room, even looked in
the bathroom medicine cabinet and the clothes hamper.

"It's just not in the house," she kept saying to Claude in a lost
way. After another day of searching, she gave up.

Claude heard her telling the woman in the next apartment
about it.

"You remember it, I suppose. I think I once showed it to you
when we had coffee and cake here."

"Yes, I do remember. That's too bad," said the neighbor.

Margaret told the news-store man, too. It embarrassed Claude painfully as he stood there staring at the rows of candy bars and Margaret said hesitantly to the man she'd hardly dared to speak to before, "I did mean to pay our bill yesterday, but I've been a little distracted. I lost a very old keepsake—an old piece of silver I was very fond of. A baby spoon."

Then at the phrase "an old piece of silver," Claude realized. *Winston* had taken it. Winston might have thought it had some value, or he might have taken it out of malice. He could have palmed it that last night he was at the house. Claude smiled to himself.

Claude had known for years that Winston stole little things— a glass paperweight, an old cigarette lighter that didn't work, a photograph of Claude. Until now, Winston had chosen Claude's possessions. For sentimental reasons, Claude thought. Claude suspected that Winston had a vaguely homosexual attachment to him, and Claude had heard that homosexuals were apt to take something from someone they cared for. What then was more likely than that Winston would take an intimate possession or two from him, which he probably made a fetish of?

Three more days passed without the spoon's turning up, and without a word from Winston. Margaret wrote some letters in the evenings, and Claude knew she was saying in each and every one of them that she had lost her baby spoon and that it was unfor-givably careless of her. It was like a confession of some terrible sin that she had to make to everyone. And more, she seemed to want to tell everyone, "Here I stand, bereft." She wanted to hear their words of comfort, their reassuring phrases about such things hap-pening to everybody. Claude had seen her devouring the sympa-thy the delicatessen woman had offered her. And he saw her anxiety in the way she opened the letter from her sister in Staten Island. Margaret read the letter at the table, and though it didn't say anything about the baby spoon, it put Margaret in better spirits, as if her sister's not mentioning it were a guarantee of her absolution.

Leonard George and his wife Lydia came to dinner one evening, and Margaret told them about the spoon. Lydia, who was by no means stupid but very good at talking about nothing, went on and on about how disquieting the losses of keepsakes were at first, and how unimportant they seemed later. Margaret's face grew gradually less troubled until finally she was smiling. After dinner, she said on her own initiative, "Well, who wants to play some bridge?"

Margaret put on a little lipstick now when they sat down to dinner. It all happened in about ten days. The inevitable pardons she got from people after confessing the loss of her baby spoon seemed to be breaking the barriers between herself and the adult world. Claude began to think he might never see that horrible coyness again when young men came to semester teas. He really ought to thank Winston for it, he supposed. It amused him to think of grasping Winston's hand and thanking him for relieving the household of the accursed baby spoon. He would have to be careful how he did it, because Winston didn't know that he knew about his petty thieveries. But perhaps it was time Winston did. Claude still resented Winston's money-begging and that shocking moment of rudeness the last time he had visited. Yes, Winston wanted bringing into line. He would let Winston know he knew about the spoon, and he would also let him have three hundred dollars.

Winston hadn't yet called, so Claude wrote a note to him, inviting him to dinner Sunday night, and saying he was prepared to lend him three hundred dollars. "Come early so we can have a little talk first," Claude wrote.

Winston was smiling when he arrived, and he was wearing a clean white shirt. But the white collar only accented the grayness of his face, the shadows in his cheeks.

"Working hard?" Claude asked as they went into his study.

"You bet," Winston said. "I want to read you a couple of pages about the subway ride Jake takes." Jake was the main character in Winston's book.

Winston was about to begin reading, when Margaret arrived with a shaker of whiskey sours and a plate of canapés.

"By the way, Winston," Claude began when Margaret had left. "I want to thank you for a little service I think you rendered the last time you were here."

Winston looked at him. "What was that?"

"Did you see anything of a silver spoon, a little silver baby spoon?" Claude asked him with a smile.

Winston's eyes were suddenly wary. "No. No, I didn't."

Winston was guilty, and embarrassed, Claude saw. Claude laughed easily. "Didn't you take it, Winston? I'd be delighted if you did."

"Take it? No, I certainly didn't." Winston started towards the cocktail tray and stopped, frowning harder at Claude, his stooped figure rigid.

"Now look here—" Why had he begun it before Winston had had a couple of cocktails? Claude thought of Winston's hollow stomach and felt as if his words were dropping into it. "Look here, Winston, you know I'm terribly fond of you."

"What's this all about?" Winston demanded, and now his voice shook and he looked completely helpless to conceal his guilt. He half turned round and turned back again, as if guilt pinned his big shoes to the floor.

Claude tipped his head back and drank all his glass. He said with a smile, "You know I know you've taken a few things from me. It couldn't matter to me less. I'm glad you wanted to take them, in fact." He shrugged.

"What things? That's not true, Claude." Winston laid his sprawling hand over the conch shell on the bookcase. He stood upright now, and there was something even militant about his tall figure and the affronted stare he gave Claude.

"Winston, have a drink." Claude wished now that he hadn't begun it. He should have known Winston wouldn't be able to take it. Maybe he had destroyed their friendship—for nothing. Claude wondered if he should try to take it all back, pretend he had been joking. "Have a drink," he repeated.

"But you can't accuse me of being a thief!" Winston said in a horrified tone. And suddenly his body began trembling.

"No, no, you've got the whole thing wrong," Claude said. He walked slowly across the room to get a cigarette from the box on his desk.

"That's what you said, isn't it?" Winston's voice cracked.

"No, I didn't. Now let's sit down and have a drink and forget it." Claude spoke with elaborate casualness, but he knew it sounded patronizing just the same. Maybe Winston *hadn't* stolen the spoon: after all, it belonged to Margaret. Maybe Winston was reacting with guilt because he had taken other things, and he now knew that Claude realized it.

That was his last thought—that he had sounded false and patronizing, that the spoon might have disappeared by some means other than Winston—before the quick step behind him, the brief whir of something moving fast through the air, and the shattering impact at the back of his head caused his arms to fling up in a last empty, convulsive gesture.

Broken Glass

Andrew Cooperman felt in a cheerful mood on a certain Wednesday morning, because he had a date. He was to ring Kate Wynant's doorbell a little after ten, and they were going to shop at the supermarket together. They did this once a week, avoiding Saturday because of the crowds, and they shopped together, because these days you couldn't buy one pound or six of anything, you had to buy five pounds of onions or ten pounds of potatoes, as if one had an army at home to feed, and Andrew lived alone, as did Kate. Andrew's wife Sarah had died nearly six years ago, and Kate's husband Al, who had been a subway guard, had passed away with bronchitis and pneumonia the year before Sarah. The Coopermans and the Wynants had been good friends and neighbors for more than thirty years. The Wynants had no children, but Andrew and Sarah had one son who had lived in New Jersey with his wife and son until ten years ago, when the family had moved to Dallas. Eddie was a good boy—Andrew's son—but not much for writing letters, two a year were about it, and one of those around Christmas. Andrew admitted to himself that he felt lonely sometimes.

And he had to admit that it was absurd to feel elated at the prospect of a date with old Kate, who would very likely have a new tale of horror for him, something else "atrocious" or "inhuman" that had happened in their Brooklyn neighborhood. Kate was on her phone half the time, people calling her or she calling them. She knew everything that was happening. Well, the neighborhood had gone down, to put it mildly. People on welfare were moving in, along with the kids that went with them. The neighborhood had used to be one of the best, lots of privately owned houses, well kept with trees and bushes and polished brass door knockers to brighten the scene. Everybody knew everybody, helped with the snow shoveling, visited at one another's birthday parties, weddings. Now with more people, and the owners dying out, the houses had had to be broken up into apartments, you couldn't do anything about that. Andrew and Sarah had always lived in the apartment Andrew had now, but once they had known the owners, the Kneses, older than he and Sarah, and long dead now. Andrew knew the owner of his four-apartment house only by name, couldn't even remember what he looked like . . . Andrew's thoughts trailed off. He glanced at his watch—five past ten—and wondered if he had forgotten anything. Money and keys, always the essentials, plus his shopping list. Yes, he had them.

Next to Andrew's apartment door, pushed against it, stood a big pine crate full of books and old magazines. That was Kate's idea, to have not only three locks plus a bolt and chain on the door, but a heavy object or two against the door. Anybody could open locks these days, said Kate, and cut through a chain quick as a wink, but if they had to do all that plus push something heavy out of the way, it would give Andrew time to use his telephone. Kate could of course tell a story or two about a woman or man whose life had probably been saved and whose possessions certainly had by this precaution. Andrew tugged at his crate, got it just far enough away that he could open his locks and squeeze out himself. Then he relocked his door, turning his keys twice. At the end of his shopping list, he had a pleasant item to acquire, a rectangular piece of glass of which he had noted the measurements. Andrew was quite a good framer, and sometimes his neighbors, like the Vernons and the Schroeders, brought him photographs and drawings to frame, and of course he didn't charge anything except the cost of his materials. Occasional framing and his own watercolors occupied much of Andrew's time. He had two portfolios of his watercolors, mostly what one might call landscapes of local parks and houses. He showed them to Kate when she asked to see his latest efforts. Two or three were framed in his apartment. Andrew frequently went through his portfolios and threw out the ones he considered not so good. No use hanging on to everything, as a lot of old people did.

Andrew had remounted his favorite photograph of Sarah, had bought a frame secondhand and spruced it up—nice bird's-eye

maple—and this evening he intended to fix the glass in the frame
and seal the back with brown paper, and hang it in his living room.
Andrew had used to be a typesetter for a Brooklyn newspaper, and
he appreciated precision, the loose but reliable bang and flop and
jangle of huge printing machines. Sometimes in dreams Andrew
heard the machines, almost smelled their oil, though even when he
had stopped working fifteen years ago, the presses had been modernized and much quieter.

"That you, Andrew?" Kate's voice shrilled down the stairs seconds after he had pushed the bell.

"Me, Kate!" he called back.

"Down in a minute!"

The door behind Andrew, the unlocked front door, suddenly
burst open and two, no three children bumped past him. One of
them had a key, and they went screaming in, one black and two
white, Andrew noticed. There was another apartment besides
Kate's on the first floor.

Kate opened the door, nearly as wide as the doorway herself, her pinkish face framed in the black fur of her coat collar.
Kate's chubby hands clutched one shopping bag of blue plastic,
plus her carrier which rolled on two wheels but was now flat
and collapsed. "What a morning! Did Ethel call you about the
Schroeders?" she asked in an unusually upset whisper.

"No, she didn't." Ethel was a neighbor, another great telephone user. Andrew supposed that the Schroeders had suffered
another house robbery.

Kate descended her front steps and got her breath back. She
planted a hand on Andrew's jacket sleeve. "They were found this
morning in their apartment—both dead from sleeping pills. They
left a note. *Suicides!*"

"No!" said Andrew, shocked. "Why?"

"They said—" Kate looked around her as if any ears might be
enemies "—they couldn't take another robbery. They were too
unhappy to go on. They'd had three or four, you know—"

"That's sad news, sad." Andrew felt that he was not taking it in as yet.

"Two burglaries just in the last six months. Remember, Andy? And Herman's back killing him since that last rip-off—when was it? December? It was cold then, anyway, I remember."

"Yes." Herman Schroeder had been taking some sun on a bench a couple of streets away—against Kate's advice, Andrew remembered, because few people were around on cold days—and a couple of boys had taken Herman's money plus his wristwatch and his winter coat. It wasn't so much what they took as the shock of it, and the boys had sat Herman down on the pavement. The benches might as well be traps, for the elderly, anyway. Once they'd all gone to the little park there, played chess and checkers in summer, but no more. Andrew could remember Herman sitting with his white pipe in the sun there, reading his newspaper. Gone now. The Schroeders were a decent couple and had been neighbors for decades, like himself and Kate. It was sinking in. "Killed themselves." He and Kate were moving in the direction of the big avenue and the supermarket.

"They couldn't afford to move anywhere else. I remember Minnie saying that to me—oh, a couple of years ago." Kate had already slowed her walk to spare her bad arches.

Across the street Andrew saw the reassuring figures of two policemen, burly fellows, swinging their sticks, and at the same time he noticed four Hispanic boys coming towards him and Kate on the sidewalk, yelping in Spanish, jostling one another, and one had the glazed look of someone drugged—or was Andrew mistaken? One boy shouted a dirty phrase in English, shoved another who bumped into Andrew, and Andrew caromed into Kate. Andrew righted himself, touched Kate's arm apologetically, but didn't bother saying "Sorry." It was as if he and she were observing a respectful silence for a few minutes in memory of Herman and Minnie Schroeder, even as they made their way to the supermarket.

Andrew said he had to buy a piece of glass, and stepped into the hardware store near the corner. He knew Kate would be content to follow him and look around at kitchen gadgets. Andrew read out his measurements, which the young man noted on a scrap of paper.

" 'Bout fifteen minutes," the young man said.

"I'll be a little longer. Going to the supermarket. Thank you." Andrew made his way towards Kate. The shop glittered with chromium toasters, grills, electric machines of all kinds.

In the supermarket they separated as usual, having established that Andrew would buy the staples, potatoes, coffee, bread and such like, while Kate got the meat and chose whatever fruit and vegetables looked good. Andrew was thinking about the Schroeders. Lots of times he and Kate had seen Minnie's small figure here, often in a dark purple coat, shopping alone on a midweek morning, and they had always paused a minute to chat and to ask how everybody was. Herman had never given up his walks, though of course he'd taken them only in daylight hours, but even so— "They prey on the elderly, because they know we can't run or hit back," Kate had said many a time. As Andrew reached for a cardboard box of a dozen eggs, he imagined Minnie and Herman— maybe lying fully clothed on a double bed—in the apartment where Andrew had been several times. *Dead.* Couldn't stand the strain any longer. Was it right to feel so pessimistic, so hopeless, Andrew wondered. Or was it fair to ask that? They must have been too tired to try any longer. Andrew supposed one had to understand and forgive that.

The fingers of the checkout girl flew over the adding machine with an amazing quickness. Andrew didn't bother peering to see if all the figures were correct, though he knew Kate did.

Kate had already checked out and was waiting this side of the glass front doors. They added some items from Andrew's sacks to the carrier. They still had a sack each to carry.

"Bought a nice coffee ring," Kate said. "We can have some at my place, if you'd like."

"That sounds nice," said Andrew. He and Kate each climbed the stairs twice at Kate's house (one flight up) in order to transport all the sacks, while they guarded their purchases in turn in the downstairs hall. You could never tell who might dash in the front door, with a key even, and dash out again with some loot. Kate was convinced some of the kids had passkeys. Kate made Nescafé and warmed the coffee ring in the oven. Then she said, as Andrew had thought she might:

"This coffee ring reminds me of dear Minnie's, only she made better herself. I'm going to miss them, Andy—"

By then they were seated at Kate's oval table in the living room, their groceries divided in the kitchen, but the bill not yet reckoned up.

Andrew nodded solemnly. "I hope I won't have to go like *that*."

"You've had only two house robberies, isn't that it? I've had four. What've I got left?" she asked rhetorically, rolling her head back so her eyes swept the walls, the sideboard on which a green vase stood (Andrew did remember a silver tray and teapot there years ago), the old secondhand television set where—was it four or even more years ago now?—Kate had had a big new set that she had been quite proud of. Andrew did not know what to say. She had been robbed, yes, but all in all maybe her apartment looked more like a home than his own. "It's harder on a man if the wife dies first than the other way around," Kate had said to him after Sarah died. That was perhaps true. Women were better at the little things, making a house look nice. At the same time Andrew warned himself (as he always had since Sarah's death) not to start feeling sorry for himself, because that was the beginning of the end, shameful even. Yet the idea, the *image* of the Schroeders appeared to Andrew more strongly as he sat there sipping Kate's coffee and eating the cinnamon-flavored cake. They had been about seventy-six, Andrew thought, both of them. Not really ancient, was it? Andrew would be eighty-one next month.

"How were they found?" Andrew asked.

"Who?"

"The Schroeders."

"Oh. I think a neighbor on the same floor knocked a few times, then told a super or somebody—because their super doesn't live in the house. I guess the neighbor just said she was worried, because she hadn't seen them in days. They'd been there about four days, Ethel said, because one of the interns said that to somebody."

In the kitchen Andrew reckoned up their bills as best he could, looking over the two sales slips and the divided wax paper–wrapped package of two loaves of bread, the pounds of potatoes. Kate liked him to do the figuring. He arrived at nearly eighteen dollars for Kate and a little more for himself, because he was vague about one item. He reloaded two sacks for himself.

"They're *inhuman,*" Kate was saying, even the slightly frayed hem of her skirt twitching now with her anger or upsetness. "You saw that piece in *Time* a couple of months ago, remember, Andy?"

He did. Kate had passed on the magazine when she had finished it, as she often did. It had not been their Brooklyn neighborhood described in the one-and-a-half page article, but one much like it. It told of people barricading their doors at night, not daring to go out after nightfall to buy anything or to visit a friend. Roving bands of teenagers, ninety-seven percent black or Hispanic, *Time* said, made people captive in their own homes, followed people back from the bank on the days when government checks came in, in order to mug them inside their own doors.

"When civilized people like the Schroeders have to kill themselves to escape—" Kate was at a loss for words and sat down, banged her reddish wig squarely on top to make sure it was in place. "The police can't offer enough protection. How can they be everywhere? They can't!"

"But don't forget," Andrew began, happy to recall a cheerful detail, "in that same *Time* piece they showed a picture of a tall black girl escorting some old people—just like us—around their neighborhood to shop. Or maybe back from the bank, I forgot."

Kate nervously picked up a pecan from her plate and pushed it between her lips. "All right, one example, one photograph. All right if we had fifty decent young people like that around here who'd escort *all* of us . . ."

Andrew knew he had best take his leave. Kate could go on another half hour. "I thank you for the delicious coffee and cake, Kate."

"Call me tonight. I feel uneasy, Andy, don't know why. Just today especially."

He nodded. "What time?" he asked, as if making another date, and in a way it was. He liked to have things to look forward to, little duties.

"Just before eight. Five minutes to eight, all right? Because I want to watch something on TV at eight."

Andrew departed, and was all the way home, his sacks emptied and the things put away in his own kitchen, before he realized that he had forgotten to pick up the piece of glass. Now if that wasn't stupid! Sign of old age, he thought, and smiled at himself. Andrew put on his jacket again. Again he unlocked, then relocked his apartment door, thinking he had only himself to blame for this extra exertion. He walked towards the big avenue again with his rather short-stepped gait, right foot a bit slower than the other.

"Morning, Andy," said an elderly woman who had her white dog tied to her wheeled grocery carrier, now full.

"Morning—" Andrew replied, not recalling at once her name. *Helen,* of course, now that it was too late to say it. Helen *Vernon.*

Andrew entered the hardware shop and claimed his glass. Two dollars and eighty-eight cents. The glass was neatly wrapped in brown paper, Scotch-taped. Andrew started home with the glass under his arm. He looked forward to a happy evening of puttering in the little spare room which had used to be Sarah's sewing and ironing room and where Andrew had always had his workbench, which was a flush door on a trestle. The sun had come out brighter now. Andrew glanced up and saw a helicopter pulling a streamer with something written on it that he could not read. A twist of smoke rose from someone's back garden: twigs being burnt. The air promised spring.

He heard rather quick steps behind him, and instinctively moved to the right to let someone pass him on the street side, then got a forceful jolt against his left arm under which he carried the glass. Andrew was knocked to the right, knocked off his feet, and he heard the glass strike the sidewalk with a *clink,* and at the same time Andrew's right hip gave a crack.

Andrew saw blue-jeaned legs, heard gasping as his jacket was wrenched backward, as a button leapt under his nose, and his arms were suddenly pinned to his sides. Now his hat was off, and Andrew expected a blow on the head, but instead a black hand tore his wallet out of the inside pocket of his jacket. Andrew blinked, saw big sneakered feet, long legs in blue jeans, blue denim jacket above, loping away up the sidewalk, turning right at the next corner.

Seconds later, almost at once, a woman bent over him, having come from behind him. "I *saw* that!" she said.

She was trying to help him up, and Andrew got on his knees, hampered by the jacket which still bound his arms. The woman— her head wrapped in a blue scarf, her shopping bag on the sidewalk—held his arm out and pulled up his jacket collar so that the jacket was on his shoulders again. He took her extended hand, and then he was up, on his feet.

"I do thank you," Andrew said, "very much."

"You think you're all right?" She looked in her forties, anxious now, and hair curlers showed under the scarf.

Andrew was much relieved to find that he could stand on his legs without pain. He had feared a hip fracture. "I thank you," he repeated, and realized he was dazed.

"Those *animals*! If I could just see a cop—" She looked all around, gave it up for the moment. "I'll make sure you get home. Where do you live? Want a taxi?"

"No, no, very near."

They began to walk. The nice woman held his arm. She went on talking:

". . . 'course you never see a cop when you need one . . . one of the old people in my house just last week. Do they think they can take over this neighborhood? Hah! They'd better think *again* . . . And what do they want, when you come down to it, recreation halls they've already got, unemployment pay, welfare, a *salary* if they just go to a training school! . . . Public libraries! But do you see 'em in the library here? No, they'd rather spend their time robbing . . . Do these apes think we didn't *work* for what little we've got? . . . Got a son. He talks about us getting guns the way they do in San Francisco or is it Los Angeles? . . . Lookit this, no cop yet!"

"Here's where I live," Andrew said when they came to a two-story red brick and creamy cement house.

The woman offered to help him up the stairs, but Andrew said he could make it alone.

"How much did you lose by the way?" she asked.

Andrew tried to think. "Not more than ten dollars. I don't—" He stopped and began again. "It's identification cards and such. I'll write for some more. Got the numbers—"

"If you tell me your name, I'll report this to the police. I saw that tall boy—"

"Oh, no, no. Thank you," said Andrew rather firmly, as if her reporting the matter might be somehow in his disfavor.

"Take care. Bye-bye," said the woman, and went off in the direction they had come from.

Andrew made his way upstairs, fished keys from his trousers pocket, entered, relocked his door, and slowly prepared a pot of tea. Tea was always the best after a shock. He had to admit he'd had a shock. Yes. Even though this was the second or third time, the last having been more than a year ago—But this one in broad daylight, high noon! Andrew put two spoonfuls of sugar in his tea, and sat down at the kitchen table. At least his groceries were here at home safe. And his hip was not hurting much, just a little pain like a bruise. Just suppose he'd broken his hip, couldn't walk for the next two or three months, dependent on Kate to buy his food? Now that would've been catastrophic! Andrew felt grateful to fate.

He made a peanut butter sandwich, could eat only half of it, and suddenly realized that he needed to lie down. He pushed off his shoes and lay down on the living room couch, pulled up the crocheted coverlet that Sarah had made. It seemed to Andrew that he'd hardly begun to doze off, when the telephone rang. Probably Kate.

And Kate it was, saying the funeral for the Schroeders was Saturday at 11 A.M., and would Andrew like to come, because there was a small bus that several of the neighbors intended to take to go to the cemetery.

"Why, yes—sure," Andrew said, feeling it was a neighborly duty to go, a sign of his respect that he would be glad to make.

"Fine, Andy. I'll ring your bell around ten-fifteen Saturday because you're on the way. How you feeling? There's a documentary on TV tonight that might interest you. Nine o'clock, if that isn't too late. Till ten but—We *could* meet half way and sort of walk each other, but I suppose it's silly to take a chance just for a TV program."

It was silly, was Andrew's opinion at the moment, though he said nothing.

"Still there, Andy?—Are you okay?"

"Well, since you ask," Andrew replied, "I just got mugged, sat down on the—"

"Why didn't you tell me right away? I knew something would happen today! Did they hurt you?"

"Just one boy. No, I'm all right, Kate."

"Which one was it? D'you get a look at him?"

"Oh, yes. Tall black fellow with a little red in his hair."

"Maybe I know the one you mean. Not sure though. You went out again, Andy?"

"Forgot that piece of glass. Had to go back for it."

They agreed that Andrew shouldn't go out again today after dark, because lightning did sometimes strike the same place twice.

Then Andrew went back to the living room couch which, sagging though it was, he had always loved to snooze on. He quickly became drowsy again, but his half-sleep was troubled. He felt melancholic too, because he did not want to go out again, and this evening he would not have the glass he needed to frame the photograph of Sarah. What would happen to all those glass shards on the sidewalk which he'd been too upset to pick up? Would some other kids pick them up, make use of them against the local people? Andrew squirmed on the couch. The boys mostly carried knives, easier to handle. The first time Andrew had been ripped off, the time they got his leather wallet (after that he used plastic wallets), a younger boy had stood in front of him with a knife at the level of Andrew's eyes as he sat on the pavement, while an older boy had lifted his wallet. From beyond his apartment door, Andrew heard the clicking of locks, the slide of a bolt. Mrs. Wilkie was going out.

Tomorrow he'd acquire another piece of glass, and tomorrow evening or even afternoon he'd have the pleasure of hanging the photograph, and of seeing Sarah's gently smiling face as she had looked at twenty-five or -six—when Eddie had been about two—wearing the summer dress that was cut low in front with ruffles, and the coral necklace Andrew had given her. Andrew felt old. When he thought of all those *years*! To feel old was mainly to feel tired, he supposed. Maybe it was inevitable, for everyone. He had been lucky in the sense of being healthier than most people, free of rheumatism and the usual complaints. What depressed him, he realized, was the prospect of the grave, of death soon. Death would be perhaps merely a moment, maybe quite painless, but it was also a mystery. Was it just like fainting? Andrew still found life interest-

ing enough to want to go on living. Day after tomorrow, he'd
attend the funeral of Herman and Minnie Schroeder, and in a few
years from now, maybe very few years, other neighbors like Kate
and Helen Vernon would be attending *his* funeral. People like
Kate would mention him in the months that followed, say perhaps
that they missed him, and then they would stop mentioning him,
as people would the Schroeders finally. What was life all about? It
seemed to Andrew that there ought to be something more to hang
onto, more to represent a man, even the humblest, than a few sticks
of furniture, a few dollars in the bank, some old books and photographs, when he died. *Dust unto dust,* Andrew thought and
turned over on his side, whereupon his bruised hip began to hurt,
but he lay still, too tired to change his position. Of course there
was his son Eddie, and his son Andy, a grown-up man of twenty-
eight now himself. But what Andrew was thinking about was
something personal and individual to him: what was he worth, as
a human being?

So Andrew did not go to Kate's that evening, but made a supper of macaroni and cheese (not frozen, it was cheaper to make it
himself) and a green salad. After his supper, he pulled out a kitchen
drawer and reached behind the plastic tray, which contained
knives, forks, and spoons, for his spare money, lest he go out and
be down on the street tomorrow before he realized that he hadn't
money. Andrew took four singles, which left a fiver in the drawer,
and put them into his trousers pocket. Then he wrote his letters of
notice of stolen cards to his bank and to the Social Security office.

The next morning, a lovely sunny morning, Andrew went
again to the hardware store and put in his order for a piece of glass
measuring twenty-four by eighteen inches. Andrew had expected
the young man to say, "Broke it?" or something like that, in which
case Andrew would have smiled and said yes, but the young man
was too busy to say anything but "Fifteen minutes."

Fifteen minutes could pass quickly for Andrew in a hardware
shop, so he browsed among hammers and wrenches, potato-

peelers, coffee-makers which kept the pot warm on a little platform after it was done, fancy hooks for bathroom walls, bags of
peat and supercharged humus for the garden, charcoal broilers of
various heights and diameters, and then the young man was standing by him with the glass all wrapped again, and looking the same
as yesterday's package. Andrew again paid two dollars and eighty-
eight cents to the girl cashier. Andrew thought he would frame the
picture before lunch. The picture might inspire him to call up Kate
and invite her to tea. Kate liked tea with dainty but substantial ham
and mayonnaise sandwiches, for instance, followed by a cake.
Andrew might shop for all that after lunch.

Andrew had entered the second block of his three-block walk
home, when he saw the same black boy in the same blue denim
jacket approaching him, hands in his back pockets, whistling,
swinging his feet out like a sailor.

Andrew stiffened. Did the boy recognize him? But the boy
wasn't even looking at him. Same reddish black kinky hair, over six
feet tall, yes, same boy. What had he bought with the ten dollars,
Andrew wondered, at the same time noticing that the unbuttoned
denim jacket sparkled with what seemed to be bottle caps fixed up
and down the front. Who was he going to rip off next, this noon
or later? These thoughts or impressions flashed through Andrew's
mind in seconds, and then the big, freckled eyes of the boy met
Andrew's, sharp but empty of recognition, and his figure came on,
sure that Andrew would step aside for him. His hands and arms
swung free now, maybe ready to give Andrew a shock by spreading out, as if he intended to crash into Andrew.

Now Andrew's right hand clenched the bottom of his package more firmly, tilted a corner forward as if it were a lance, and
Andrew did not step aside. He simply kept his course—as the boy's
arms flew out to make him jump—braced his body for an impact,
and saw the point of the package hit near the white buttons on the
pale blue shirt.

"*Ow!*"

The jolt sent Andrew backward, but he kept his footing.

"Oooh," the boy groaned more gently, and folded his hands over his stomach. "Son of a *bitch*!" Blood oozed over his clasped fingers.

A man appeared on the sidewalk behind Andrew. A woman with a shopping carrier like Kate's had come from the opposite direction and hesitated with her mouth slightly open.

"He stab me!" the boy whined in falsetto. He was bent double, leaning against a fire hydrant.

The man, who carried a lot of cardboard sheets under one arm, looked more curious than concerned. "What happened? Another boy?" he asked Andrew.

"He *stab* me!"

Neither the man nor the woman paid any attention to that.

". . . find a doctor?" the woman was saying vaguely to the man.

"Better find one. Yeah. Maybe," said the man, and went on his way.

The woman made a sound like "Tschuh!" and took two drifting steps away, plainly wanting to quit the scene. "They *live* like that," she said to Andrew, flinging out one hand for emphasis. "They do it to us and once in a while *they* get it." She hurried off, but turned back to say, "If I see a policeman . . ." She went on.

The boy looked at Andrew, muttered something that sounded like a threat, and here came his chums, two or three of them, Andrew walked on towards his house. The padding of sneakers, of leaping feet crossed the street, and Andrew saw one of the figures dodge a passing car. A corner of Andrew's glass package hung limp. He had really given the boy a slash. Andrew thought of rapes in his neighborhood (not always reported in the newspapers, he and Kate had noticed), in which the girl had suffered a knife wound in the cheek lest she scream, plus the insult of rape. He realized that his heart was thumping with anger, with fear too. He had meant to strike back. Well, he had. Let the police come, let them accuse him, charge him. Maybe they would. Andrew thought they might.

It was not until he had set the glass package down and was tackling his apartment door's three locks that Andrew noticed the fingers of his right hand were bleeding on the inside. Part of the brown paper was sodden with blood. Andrew went into his apartment and locked his door from inside again, letting the blood fall on the brown package which he had laid flat on the floor. Then carefully, so as not to drip on the hall carpet, Andrew held his right wrist and got to the kitchen which was closer than the bathroom. He ran cold water over his hand. The cuts were not bad, he thought, wouldn't need stitches anyway, just a few Band-Aids. He pushed the crate of books and magazines back against the door.

By two o'clock that afternoon Andrew was feeling better, though around noon he had had some bad moments. One finger had refused to stop bleeding for quite a while, then Andrew had made some lunch, and had lain down on the living room couch, feeling weak. Just after two he put on his jacket and went out again to buy his piece of glass. This time the same young man—who knew Andrew slightly because of Andrew's purchases of glass for pictures in the past—did make a remark, smiling a little, and Andrew, not having caught every word of what he said, replied, "Yes—got a couple of pictures same size to do." Andrew again waited, and when he got the glass, proceeded to the main avenue, where there was a bakery between the subway entrance and the public library. Andrew wished he had brought his books, not yet due, but he had read them and might have changed them. At the bakery, he bought a three-layer chocolate cake with white icing plus some brown-edged cookies. Then he walked home the way he had come, his usual route, past the spot where he had encountered the boy today, though he did not glance to his left where he might have seen blood stains. Andrew did not look around him at all, though he imagined, he felt sure, that the tall boy's chums were going to be on the lookout for him. From now on, to go out of his house would be to take more of a risk than usual.

At home again, he was conscious of taking another small risk when he telephoned Kate before he had framed the photograph, because the photograph in its frame was part of his tea invitation. Kate was in and said she would love to come over around four.

Andrew got busy. He had wrapped a clean rag around his right hand, which made him a little clumsy, but he worked carefully. One sweep of blood, crescent-shaped, got on the brown paper that Andrew had neatly sealed on the back of the frame, but that couldn't be helped, because he hadn't wanted to spend time changing the bandage. He put in the screw eyes and attached the brass picture wire for hanging. Then Andrew did change the bandage, keeping the Band-Aids on, and with his left hand hammered the nail into the wall for the picture, and put the picture up.

Now that looked beautiful! He straightened the picture delicately with one finger. Sarah brightened his whole living room, made a tremendous change. She smiled out at him, her head slightly turned but her eyes direct, and he imagined he could hear her saying, "Andy." Andrew smiled back at her, and for several seconds felt young, felt as if he were breathing the crisp air that one breathed on hills in the country. Ah, well! Tea!

Andrew got out cups and saucers and plates, making sure he took ones that weren't nicked. Sugar and a little pitcher of milk. By the time he had things ready and had lit the gas under the kettle, his doorbell rang.

"Hello, Andy, and how're you feeling today?" Kate asked as she came in, puffing a little from the stairs.

For the moment, Andrew was keeping his right hand behind his back. "Well enough, thank you, Kate. And yourself?" He relocked the door.

"Oh-h—" Kate was unbuttoning her coat over her rather vast front, turning round as she usually did to survey the living room. She spotted the new picture on the wall. "Why, that's lovely, Andy!" She went closer. "Sarah's just lovely there! And that bird's-eye maple!"

Andrew had waxed the frame. He felt a glow of satisfaction.

Kate chattered on, recalling when they were younger, when all four of them had shared Christmas and Thanksgiving dinners and once in a while had gone out to a nearby Polish restaurant (long closed) where couples of all ages had used to dance rather sedately between courses, having a grand time. But before he had poured the tea, Kate noticed his hand.

"Cut it framing the photograph," Andrew said. "Clumsy of me. It's not serious." If he told the truth, Kate would say something alarming—Andrew didn't know exactly what, but it would have to do with the gang's hitting back, maybe all the roving gangs and there were three, one Hispanic, one black, one sort of mixed with an odd white or two. Kate might insist that he stay in for the next days while she brought him whatever he might need.

"You're sure we shouldn't look at it again while I'm here?" Kate asked through a mouthful of chocolate cake. "I can do a neat bandage for you. You can't tie a bandage with one hand. Have you got antiseptic? Alcohol?"

"Oh, Kate!"

Then inquiries about his papers, if he had written for new cards. Andrew said he had. He heated more water.

Kate insisted, before she left, on changing his bandage and tying a clean one properly. "It's just silly to stay all night with that one damp already." She had washed up the tea things, so Andrew would not get his hand wetter.

So Andrew let her undo the bandage with the aid of scissors. When she saw that four fingers had been cut, she was amazed.

"Well, it didn't happen the way I told it," Andrew said. "I— This morning I saw this same tall fellow coming at me again—just to scare me out of his way as usual, I suppose, but I didn't step out of his way, I let him walk right into the glass—point." There it was plain, and as they stood by the kitchen sink, Andrew glanced at Kate's face for shock, understanding maybe, for sympathy too.

"And you hurt him? Cut him, I mean?"

"Yes, I did." Andrew said. "He came straight at me to scare me, you know, that's why *he* didn't get out of the way one bit. But what I was carrying wasn't exactly a sack of eggs! I saw his stomach bleeding." Andrew told her about the man and woman stopping, and said maybe they had found a doctor somewhere, but Andrew had walked on home. Andrew realized he was boasting a bit, like a small boy who had done something courageous. In fact, Andrew admitted to himself that he *hoped* he had given the boy a bad cut, and a wound like that in the stomach might be fatal, Andrew thought.

"I wonder that you got home alive! What about his pals?"

"He was by himself," Andrew said, avoiding Kate's eyes. He wasn't going to say that he thought a couple of the boy's pals had seen him. Anyway the injured boy was going to tell his chums.

Kate had more questions. How badly did he think the so-and-so was hurt? Andrew said he couldn't say. Andrew said he had just wanted to stand up for people's rights to walk on the sidewalk without having to jump aside like scared rabbits for neighborhood hoodlums.

But Kate's plump, creased face still looked uneasy, she talked about getting penicillin powder for his fingers, about being afraid to take the Band-Aids off to change them. She said she would ring him later tonight, around nine, to see how he felt. Then she left.

As Andrew had supposed, Kate had told him he had better not go out of the house for the next couple of days, that she would find out by telephone what he needed and bring it to him. Andrew hadn't remonstrated, but he didn't want to be a semi-invalid, dependent upon Kate.

The next morning, Andrew found a letter from his son Eddie in his mail box. That was nice. Andrew read most of it, standing in the area between the unlocked front door and the door into his house. Eddie was well and so was Betty, his wife, and they had rented a cottage on the coast in South Carolina for a month this summer, and would Andrew like to join them for a week or two in June? Andrew at once asked himself, did they really mean it, really want him? Of course there was time to think about it, to read Eddie's typewritten letter more carefully when he got home. Now Andrew needed, besides a little fresh air, a container of cottage cheese and a jar of mayonnaise. He intended to buy those at the delicatessen instead of the supermarket.

Andrew walked to the big avenue, made these purchases, and was on his way home, had greeted two neighbors on the way, when he heard running footsteps behind him. Andrew moved to the right to let whoever it was pass on the street side of the pavement, then he felt a violent blow against the back of his head, just above the neck. Andrew sagged at once as if paralyzed. He was on his knees on the sidewalk when the next blow came, something like a stocking swung over his left shoulder, catching him in the left temple with a crack like an earthquake, like dynamite, a gunshot even, then came the faint padding of sneakers running away. Andrew's vision—one side of his head resting against pavement now—became gray, and the humming in his head was louder than anything else. He had a desire to vomit, couldn't, was aware of shoes, trouser legs, a woman's ankles near him, of voices which seemed to come through a thick sea, of a pair of feet that drifted away. This was their vengeance, and what could he do about it now? He had absolutely expected it, and it had come. He knew he was dying, knew if people tried to move him, as they were trying now, that it would not change anything. One died in one place or another. He was aware that he sighed, aware of a resignation like a wave of peace washing over him. He was aware of justice, of the absence of anger, aware of the value of what he had done—and done all his life, and even yesterday when he had struck a small blow in the name of his neighborhood. Kate would tell the neighbors. Kate would go to his funeral. But all that was unimportant compared to the great event happening to him, the event of dying, of stopping. What mattered justice, revenge, movement of any kind? He then reached a point of being unable to think further, and was aware of a most wonderful sense of balance.

A loud exclamation or command from one of the people lifting him was unintelligible to Andrew, like another language.

Please Don't
Shoot the Trees

"We *were* on the subject of water conservation in summer!" a voice screamed. "Just in principle!"

"We never finished the *fish*!" cried another voice, even shriller.

"Who's the chair today?"

"And the *trees* . . ." That voice faded off.

Elsie Gifford smiled, sighed, but was sufficiently interested to rise a little in her chair and look behind her to identify, if possible, the ones who were crying out. She had come to listen today, not having any particular problem at the moment.

"Be damned to you all!"

Laughter! That had been a hell of a voice.

Elsie laughed too. This would be something to tell Jack about tonight—though Jack thought Citizens for Life a silly organization. Elsie and Jack, like most of the people at the meeting, lived in a protected residential area called Rainbow, far enough south of Los Angeles to be free of smog. Los Angeles, in fact, was now abandoned by industry and residents, yet poor people still lived there. "The better-off" were doing their own fighting back now, thrusting their protected areas farther into the cesspools of such cities as Los Angeles, Detroit and Philadelphia. Now it was the underprivileged, the poor, forced to move ever closer together in the cities, because they had nowhere else to go. Everything had become so tidy, nobody could even go camping any more, park a trailer anywhere, or even sleep in the woods.

"The *trees*!" the same voice was shrieking again, and she was being shouted down.

What was that tree rumor, anyway? Elsie leaned towards a woman on her left, whom she knew by sight but whose name she had forgotten. "What's the business about trees?"

But her last words were drowned out.

The back doors—rather the front doors some distance behind Elsie—had burst open. A chorus of voices screamed:

"The Forty-Niners are here!"

More laughter! Lots of groans. Boos, even.

"Get them *out*!"

But there was a patter of applause too.

Elsie smiled again, because she had been thinking that this was all the meeting needed—the Forty-Niners. They were a group of teenagers (average age nineteen, Elsie remembered) who used a covered wagon as their emblem, and aimed to make the West, chiefly California or the Golden Gate, as pure as it had been, presumably, back in 1849, the year of the Gold Rush. Jack laughed at them, because the men of the Gold Rush era had not been particularly pure in spirit, and hadn't used covered wagons to get to California, just ponies, stagecoaches and shoe leather. But this was 2049, so the kids had hitched onto the date.

Now the youngsters were streaming down the aisle, holding aloft a banner ten feet long—or three meters—fixed to two poles, with a brown covered wagon painted on it and the words: KEEP THE WEST GOLDEN!

"Halt nuclear tests! Halt nuclear *reactors*!"

"You can stop them! You *women*! And *men*!"

"Many of you are married to men making these nukes!"

". . . which are shattering the foundations of your own houses!" Several girls' voices came out clearest.

The Forty-Niners were always well-rehearsed. They kept their numbers around two hundred. They were a self-styled elite.

"An earthquake is fore-*CAST*! An earthquake is fore-*CAST*!" chanted the Forty-Niners.

Some rather senior citizens had folded their arms, smiling indulgently, but with an air of surrender. The meeting was finished, as far as scheduled agenda went. The Forty-Niners always took from five to seven minutes to make their point, then departed, but so many people had to get home or to work (there were so many job shifts now), that the agenda could never be resumed.

". . . ABOLISH *NUKES*!"

What would Jack shout back if he were here, Elsie wondered.

Jack was a physicist, and considered nuclear energy the greatest boon to mankind ever invented, or discovered, by technologists. He would certainly remind these kids that the Rainbow scientists had extinguished an awful holocaust, that had been melting a nuke, by means of chemicals that had been right on hand, as demanded by law. Lots of people were leaving now, Elsie saw. She got up too.

"Aren't they loudmouths!" This was from Jane Newcombe, a blondish woman of Elsie's age, a neighbor.

Elsie smiled more broadly. "But they *mean* well," she replied, laying on the tongue-in-cheek tolerance, playing it safe. "Can I give you a lift home, Jane?"

"Thanks, I came in my own copter. How's everything?"

"Oh, as usual. Fine," Elsie said.

Elsie climbed into her battery-run copter and rose gently straight up. At sedate speed, she turned south towards Rainbow and floated almost noiselessly towards it. On either side little red and green lights of other copters circulated like lazy butterflies, heading for labs, factories, or home. To the west on her right lay the darkness of the Pacific, bordered by a thin string of lights that marked radar stations, all laser-gun equipped, though the lights from a height looked like a carelessly tossed diamond necklace, or like something natural, anyway, due to the shoreline. She could also see the great more-than-half-circle of purple and orange lights that marked the eastern boundary of Rainbow and extended almost to the shore. Rainbow's two arcs of light were laser gadgets which could slice through anything metal, however thick, which might be flying towards Rainbow with unfriendly intent. Elsie descended, approaching her home now. Her copter, like most household copters, went only sixty kilometers per hour maximum. Such helicopters (the two for the kids had a fifty MPH maximum) were considered patriotic and conservative, because they used minimum juice and made almost no noise. They suited Elsie perfectly, though Jack sometimes griped about the low speed.

Elsie made a pass straight over their copter hangar whose roof had a scanning device. A number was written under her copter, and the roof automatically opened for her. She lowered the copter, and the automatic radar took over, parking her. Jack wasn't home yet, but the boys were, she saw from their two copters. Today had been a sports afternoon, and they had stayed until 5 P.M. at school.

Since it was already past seven, Elsie decided on a pushbutton dinner. Her U-Name-It machine held thirty-six dinners, and it was now more than half empty. One ordered an entire cylinder, glass-fronted, refrigerated, but with individual electronic heating devices to heat the section desired. There were kosher cylinders, vegetarian, diabetic, low-calorie, but the Giffords preferred the mixed, which offered four Chinese meals, four Mexican, Greek, Italian and so on.

"UNDER CONTROL," JACK Gifford said with a smile, when Elsie asked him about the earthquake rumors. "We know all about the San Andreas fault."

Elsie told him about the meeting, not that there was much to tell, because of the break-up by the Forty-Niners.

At the mention of the Forty-Niners, their son Richard, aged ten, left the table to get something, and now he was coming back with a yellow airplane made of a folded piece of paper. "They were dropping these today," Richard said.

"Oh yeah, yeah," his younger brother Charles put in. "Dropping by copter. Lots of 'em."

Elsie opened the paper airplane and read:

MESSAGE FROM THE FORTY-NINERS:

AN EARTHQUAKE

is predicted—though you'll never hear it

from the "Authorities"!

DO YOU CARE?

FIGHT NOW AGAINST NUKES AND UNDERGROUND

NUCLEAR EXPLOSIONS!

Y O U R EARTH IS TREMBLING!

TREE ROOTS ARE BEING DISTURBED!

TREES ARE DEVELOPING STRANGE DISEASES,
DYING!

DO YOU CARE? MARCH WITH US TO GOLDEN GATE
STATE CAPITOL

NEXT SATURDAY NOON!

ASSEMBLE FIRST 11 AM GOLDEN GATE TOWN HALL

(outside)

or send a donation to FORTY-NINERS

Box 435 Electron Blvd

South San. Fran. OR DO BOTH!

Jack glanced at the paper too. "Always asking for handouts,
you can bet on that. The parents ought to keep those kids at home.
South San Fran! That slum!"

Elsie remembered when she and Jack had got out in the streets
in the late thirties, before they were married, protesting—what?
Elsie had some fellow-feeling for the kids, even the Forty-Niners,
who seemed so much more militant and well-organized than any
groups she and Jack had known.

"But what is all this about an earthquake? Just not true?" Elsie
asked.

Jack put down his plastic chopsticks—it was a Chinese dinner—and replied, "First of all, not true, because we know one's not
due for years. Second, if it came, we'd have hours of warning, and
we'd control it by counterbombing underground, which would
simply drain off the strain. I explained all that to you."

Jack certainly had, and Elsie remembered. She looked at the
faces of her two sons. The boys were listening with the neutral,
vaguely amused smiles which Elsie had come to detest, smiles that
said, "Nothing's going to surprise us, because we don't give a
damn, see?" Elsie had seen the same smiles while they watched

the most horrific television programs—and also when she had informed them, about a year ago, that their grandparents, her mother and father, had been killed in a helicopter collision over Santa Fe. Something had gone wrong with the radar in the other people's copter, it had later been found. Helicopter collisions were impossible if the radar was functioning, even if one copter tried to ram another. The know-it-all, what-the-hell smiles protected Richard and Charles. Four or five years ago, when she and Jack had had the more or less usual trouble with the boy's resistance to reading and short-interest-span syndrome, the psychiatrist had called them semi-autistic, but he had also let slip out apathetic, which Elsie preferred because it was more accurate, in her opinion. Good old Greek! She had managed to take a year of Greek in university in the last year it was being taught in America. Elsie forced her eyes, with a nervous jerk of her head, away from her sons, and said, "What?" because Jack was still talking.

"Well, hon, if you're not listening—"

"I was listening."

"We've freed Golden Gate—and America, the whole *world* from the fear of earthquakes. If the bastards on the other side of the world like Italy and Japan had the dough to buy our equipment . . ."

Yes, Jack. But Elsie didn't say it. When she and Jack had been twenty-one or so, they hadn't talked like this. There had still been a hope, an intention of sharing everything with everyone, at least that intention had prevailed among lots of people besides "rabels" of which she and Jack had been two—rabels being a combination of rebel and rabble. Now America itself was partitioned into four big "states" of which Golden Gate was the richest (all of California up to Canada), and they didn't share anything with the others. The whole Western Coast was one big fortress against Sino-Russia, Japan being a demilitarized colony of theirs, Sino-Russia. The great cities had become unsupervised prisons of the poor and the black, and New York and San Francisco were dirty words, as dirty as Detroit and Philadelphia had been to Elsie's grandmother.

"And the trees, Jack. Have you heard anything about diseases? They were talking tonight—not just the Forty-Niners—"

"Nothing from our Forestry Department, hon. You know these kids ride the same old conservation jazz about spoiling nature, all that crap. Times haven't changed. If our nukes or the testing were putting us in danger of *anything,* we'd stop 'em, wouldn't we? We've got battery power in reserve everywhere." Jack exuded confidence, reassurance. Even his cheeks were rosy with health. The scientists at Jack's lab played tennis or swam three times a week, in the lab's big gymnasium.

So Elsie felt better. Jack had degrees in seismology and oceanography as well as in physics. She had graduated from a liberal arts university, and felt her own diploma to be on a par with a degree in knitting.

The next morning—a fine, sunny October morning—Elsie decided to hop over to Rainbow Library some eight miles away. She had hardly sat down in her copter when she saw more yellow papers wafting down from the sky. She got out and picked one up from the graveled driveway.

TREES BLISTERS NOW . . .
DUE TO JIGGLED SAP!
ARE YOU INTERESTED?
PROTECT YOUR TREES! PROTECT EARTH!
PROTECT YOURSELF!
BAN NUKES AND NUKE TESTS!

The rest was a repetition of time and place of the Forty-Niners' next meeting. Jiggled sap? What were they talking about? The page was badly printed as usual. Elsie got back into her copter.

There wasn't any need for Elsie to go to Rainbow Library, because audio-video books could be ordered by telephone and delivered by helicopter. Every home in Rainbow had a pick-up and delivery tower, radar-locked. But Elsie enjoyed looking at the big lighted bulletin board that reeled off new titles available, enjoyed running into friends and having a chat and a coffee on the Library grounds. The building was a vast mauve construction in the shape of RL, but joined, as in an old cattle brand, legible from the air. Elsie returned a couple of cylinders and took out three, one contemporary novel, the complete works of T. S. Eliot including his essays, and a new offering which she was lucky to get—new Chinese and Russian poems. Elsie often played these while she pottered about the house or worked in the garden. One cylinder could be of eight hours' duration. The same cylinder could be attached to the television set, and one could see the reader, plus background scenes appropriate to whatever the text was. The advantage in Elsie's opinion was that the cylinders always had the complete text of the original. They were considered classics now, slow and old-fashioned.

"Thanks, Gwyn," Elsie said to the woman behind the desk, though Elsie had got her cylinders by pushbutton. "Quiet here this morning!" Elsie hadn't met anyone she knew, or knew well enough to want to have a coffee with.

"Yes," said Gwyn. She was a woman of about forty, a health-faddist, good at sports.

It was unusual for Gwyn to be so unsmiling, and Elsie said, "Anything the matter?"

Gwyn looked for a second embarrassed, then shook her head and said, "Oh, no. Everything's under control."

Elsie thought perhaps something had happened in Gwyn's family—a death. A parent, maybe, because Gwyn was not married. Elsie went out to her copter. She was only a little distance from it when a spot on a tree trunk, at eye level, caught her attention. A funny mushroom, Elsie supposed. It was a bulging white disk and its center was slightly pink. Like a woman's breast, she thought, and repressed a giggle. She turned to her copter, and saw another larger circle on a larger tree. Fungus. That was what the Forty-Niners must mean about the trees. It didn't seem a huge problem. Rainbow had successfully fought fungi before, and they'd certainly had some odd ones.

Still, Elsie felt disturbed, and when she got home switched on the television news and listened as she deposited her library cylinders in the audio-video. The news sounded positively soothing, as usual. Elsie was about to ring U-Name-It for a refill of mixed, when the news announcer broke into a colorful smile and said, "Now for a special announcement. Please do *not* touch your trees, for any purpose, till further notice. Those funny looking growths aren't dangerous but they *can* spread, and some kids are shooting them with air rifles or poking them for fun. The Forestry Department is already taking care of them, so don't you folks worry. Forestry will make a stop at *your* house in the next forty-eight hours. But don't let the kids touch 'em. Okay, folks?" A big grin.

Elsie didn't like the sound of that. This was the local Rainbow news. She telephoned Jack, something she rarely did in working hours.

"Oh, forget it, honey! What else've they got to talk about on the news?" Jack sounded as calm as ever.

But when Elsie was looking over the U-Name-It mixed, which had been installed around 3 P.M., she noticed that the refrigerator power had automatically switched over from nuke to battery. That meant an emergency of some kind.

Elsie went at once to the telephone and rang up Jane Newcombe.

"Haven't you heard?" Jane said. "It's probably because Jack's in top-secret and sworn to silence. The trees are shooting inflammable *sap*, Elsie! Something like phosphorus or napalm. Remember napalm?"

Elsie did. "What do you mean, shooting?"

"These mushroom things explode. In fact they're not fungus. More like a cancer. Gosh, everyone's known about it for at least—

since early this morning. Kids aren't supposed to poke them, so tell your boys."

"But it's a tree disease, isn't it?"

"I dunno. What's the use of giving it a name? As you always say, Elsie, does it make things any better?" Jane tried to laugh. "If you have any on your trees, don't walk too close, dear, because they go off."

"Like guns?"

"Can't talk anymore, Tommy's just come in and I want to make sure he's briefed. Okay?"

When she had hung up, Elsie went out the rear door of the house, out a second door in the covered passage to the copter and car garage onto her driveway. She loved her poplars, the young oak, the palm trees, the two pineapple trees. Elsie tended the garden, pruned the roses, kept an eye on everything. Jack wasn't keen on gardening. She walked down the broad graveled drive to the iron gates, stood for a moment looking through the gates at the gently rolling land beyond, at the yellowish but fertile soil, at the varying green of trees and the fuzzy orange and yellow patch in the distance, a citrus orchard. Heavenly, she thought. And healthy. At least to the eye.

She began to walk back to her house. Now she caught sight of a small whitish circle on the slender trunk of the oak. A pang went through her, as if she had seen a wound on one of her own children. The white circle confronted her directly, like some kind of accusation. It was hardly three inches in diameter, smaller than the two she had seen at Rainbow Library, but unmistakably *what it was,* and she could also see a pinkness at the center.

A rifle or pistol shot made Elsie jump, her sandals rattled on the gravel, and she realized how tense she was. Their nearest neighbors, the Osbournes, sometimes shot clay pigeons. Hunting was forbidden in Rainbow. She heard two more shots, more distant, and from another direction.

The telephone was ringing. Elsie ran in and answered it eagerly.

"This is Helen Ludlow at Rainbow Academy," said a pleasant young voice. "Mrs Gifford? . . . This is just to say Richard's had a slight accident. No, not serious, I can assure you, but we're bringing him home and he may be a little late because we're—treating him. Someone will bring his copter, so he'll have it at home. His brother Charles is quite all right."

Elsie asked if it had anything to do with the trees, but the line went dead. Miss Ludlow taught history, if Elsie remembered correctly.

Now there were more gunshots, some very distant, barely audible. She went out on her driveway again to look at the spot on the oak. She imagined that it had grown larger in the last five minutes. Its outer edge was crinkled like water-soaked flesh, like something prepared to expand. It seemed to quiver as she approached. Or was she imagining?

She decided to telephone the Forestry Department.

The Forestry Department's line gave out a constant busy signal. Rainbow Hospital? She anticipated evasiveness there. The police? They would probably say it was the business of the Forestry Department. Elsie put on the television. She got a Mozart opera, on another channel a Spanish lesson, then a gymnastics class, a cooking lesson, finally came to her senses and pushed Channel 30 which gave out news twenty-four hours a day. The announcer was talking about the President's warm reception at a Far Eastern capital, as if anyone cared.

Elsie was aware of a growing panic.

She grabbed a jacket and went to her copter. At least from the copter she would be able to *see* what was happening.

The sporadic gunshots kept up.

Elsie headed in the same direction she had gone that morning, towards the center of Rainbow called the Forum, which held

the Library, Rainbow Hospital, Town Hall and Symphony Hall.
Now she noticed a more than usual number of cars on the roads,
all moving towards the eastern borders of Rainbow. They looked
like ladybirds—some of them did have polka-dot roofs—but small
as they were, they held more than most copters could, if one was
moving home. Each battery car took only two passengers, but
behind there was ample room for suitcases, crates and whatnot.
Elsie flew lower as she approached a grove of trees. She saw men
with rifles. Some were laughing, bending backward, though she
couldn't hear what they said.

"Hey! Not so close!" a man on the ground yelled at her, waving his arms.

"Vibes! Keep clear!" called another voice.

"And shut up yourself!" said the first man.

Elsie saw two trees then a third wilt rapidly, and collapse—in
a matter of ten seconds! Figures scattered away on the run.

More guns went off.

Two white ambulances rushed at top speed (they went faster
than ordinary cars, but were also on battery) towards the tree area.
Elsie cut her forward power and hovered. She was now over
another part of the park, over trees which bordered Symphony
Hall.

"Go *away* please!" That was from a middle-aged man below
who brandished a stick. "Vibrations!" He wore the dark green uniform of the Forestry Department.

Then Elsie saw a white jet come from nowhere and hit the
man in the face. The man screamed and fell, head in his hands.

At once, without even thinking, Elsie lowered her copter. The
man had fallen in a wide lane, and she had space to land. She got
out and ran the short distance to where he lay. She could hear his
groans now.

"Are you—" Elsie stopped in horror. The man's face was
burning. Steam actually rose, and she could smell it—scorched
flesh plus something aromatic, like resin. She pulled the man's

hands down instinctively from his face, then saw that his palms were burning too. "Can you walk to the copter?" Elsie looked around wildly for help, because he showed no sign of getting up, and she was not sure she could get him to the copter to fly him to the hospital a half mile away. Was this what had happened to *Richard*?

She caught the man under his arms, began to drag him towards the copter, and realized that he had fainted. No, he was dead. His eyes, open, had turned upward and were pink-white except for a crescent of gray. *Was* he dead? She bent quickly to look for a pulse in his wrist.

"Get away this place is *dangerous*!" This came from a tall, booted figure in green, another Forestry Department man, young, furious, with a rifle in his hands.

"What's *happening*?"

"We're shooting the trees and there's no telling which way they'll go off! *Take off*, ma'am!"

Elsie cast a glance around her, saw several trees wilting, heard more gunshots, then ran towards her copter. She imagined that the ground shook under her feet, but she dismissed the idea. She had just seen a man die. Why shouldn't she imagine that the ground was shaking? As she started the copter, she saw a man fire his rifle at a tree and duck at the same time, as if dodging a live enemy, and Elsie saw the jet of white sap—or something—spew like a lanced boil, except that no boil was like this. The jet had looked strong as a garden hose turned on full, like a deliberate act of retaliation by the tree.

The copter rose, and Elsie looked fixedly at the sight below. In the grove, five or six slender columns of smoke swayed in the gentle wind. The fires could get out of control, she thought. She saw a Forestry man with a rifle creeping stealthily among wilting, smoking trees, looking for another mark. A jet got him first at chest level, knocked him sideways, and Elsie saw him tearing his jacket off, saw smoke coming from the cloth of his uniform, then she had to give her attention to the copter controls. She flew homeward at top speed.

The surface of their swimming pool rippled, heaved almost, as if there was a high wind, but there was hardly any wind. *Phone Jack again,* Elsie told herself. But when she picked up the telephone, she found herself dialing Jane Newcombe's number.

There was no answer, though Elsie let it ring ten times. Maybe Jane was shopping. But a stronger feeling possessed her: the Newcombes had fled. Their family of four might have been in four of the cars she had seen this morning on the roads going out of Rainbow.

She was about to try Channel 30 again, when the chimes sounded, indicating a copter wanting to land. This was a friendly signal, activated by a visitor pushing a button in his copter. It would be Richard coming home, and Charles.

A nervous young man in white got out of the big hospital copter in the driveway. The boys' two copters were landing in the hangar. Richard was with the young man, had a light bandage round his head, but he was on his feet, walking just as usual.

"Nothing at all, Mrs. Gifford. Just a little scorch mark. We just bandaged him to make sure—antiseptics, y'know. You can take the bandage off tomorrow. Better if the air gets to it—probably."

"What happened?—Can't you tell me?" she added, because the young man was trotting back to his copter, and his colleague ran to join him from the hangar.

"We got work to do, ma'am! Your boy's okay!"

In fact both Richard and Charles had their usual smiles. Elsie found her voice and said, "Come in the house, for goodness' sake! What happened, Richard?"

"He poked a tree blister," Charles said, "with a baseball bat. It was game period, see? But we weren't supposed to touch the trees." Charles's calm smile showed a hint of enjoyment.

"I ducked but the kid behind me—" Richard finished the sentence with a brush of his palms. "He really got it right in the face. Dead. Honest it was like something on TV." He spoke with a certain earnestness, as Elsie had heard him speak on rare occasions about a TV show he had enjoyed.

"What boy?" Elsie asked.

"They're closing all the schools!" Charles said. "Closed since noon! This tree stuff's like liquid fire! You ought to see it, mom!"

Richard's mouth was still turned up at the corners.

"Does it hurt, Richard?" Elsie asked.

"It would, but they put stuff on it so it won't."

"The trees are jiggling the earth," Charles told her. "The sap is jiggling the roots, and one of the fellows said there's going to be the biggest earthquake anybody's ever seen." Despite his unwonted intensity, Charles's bland smile returned, and his lids fell halfway down, sleepily, over glazed eyes.

Elsie wondered if the kids had made up most of it. "Who told you that?"

"Look at that picture on the *wall*!" Richard said, laughing.

The heaviest picture in the living room had gone very askew. Now there was a crash of glass in the kitchen, and she went to see what had happened. A glass platter of oranges and apples had jiggled from a sideboard and fallen on the tile floor. All the glasses teetered on the edges of shelves, some tinkling together like a discordant carillon. She pushed the glasses back, knowing that the gesture was futile, absurd.

"Hey, Dad's here!" Charles yelled.

Jack had come into the living room, white-faced, but with his usual smile—almost his usual smile.

"Jack—" Elsie began.

"They call it a sap disturbance in the tree roots, hon," Jack said in a calm, deep voice. "We're trying to counteract it, so don't worry."

"Did you know we've been on battery power since—maybe this morning?" Elsie asked. She heard a faint, hollow *boom* just then, distant, and the house quivered just after the sound. That had been an underground explosion. A *scree-eech* behind her: the heavy-framed picture was falling, taking the hook from the wall.

"I know," Jack said. "I didn't bother telling you. Safety measure, battery power. We had only a week to analyze this tree sap syndrome—not long enough. It's weird. Anyway—we didn't want to alarm the public by talking about it."

"Well—am I the public?"

"Honey, we're doing all the necessary. Trust me, trust us. San Andreas isn't kicking up at all yet. Just the trees. Irregular pattern. So it's hard to counterbomb. We're busy!" Jack now looked at his sons as if suddenly aware of, or annoyed by, their presence. "Hey, Ritchie—"

"Yes," Elsie said. "He punctured a tree. He—" Suddenly Elsie realized that Jack was in a state of shock, a kind of trance. He hadn't noticed Richard's bandage until now—and now he looked at Richard with eyes as glazed as the boys' eyes. "Shouldn't we leave, Jack? Everyone's leaving, aren't they? The Newcombes have left!"

The question did not bring Jack out of his semi-trance, but he talked. They were bombing peripherally to drain the strain, he said, and why didn't they all have some instant coffee or chocolate milk instead of standing around in the living room? Another crash came from the kitchen, and Elsie paid no attention. She was hanging on her husband's words, trying to derive some comfort, even information, from them.

"Suppose the bombing just activates the sap—and San Andreas?"

The boys were now hopping about the living room, screaming with laughter, feeling furniture that was trembling and drifting.

"We just shoot 'em and they wilt, finished," Jack said. "We're in asbestos suits. This is an asbestos suit, see?" He pulled up a headgear from the back of his neck, and peered at Elsie through a transparent panel. "I should be out fighting with 'em. Got to go. But I came home to see how you were. First of all, let's take down anything that's going to fall upstairs. *I* don't want to leave our nice home, do you?"

They all climbed the stairs. All the pictures were cockeyed, and worse, a pipe had cracked in the bathroom, and water gushed, steaming, into the tub. Elsie staggered as the house shook violently under her.

Crack!

She and Jack and the kids looked up and got their faces full of sharp plastic fragments. A split at least two inches wide ran the length of the hall ceiling and disappeared over a bedroom door.

"They can't kill all the trees in half an hour!" Elsie said. "If you mean it's just the trees *doing* it—"

"It's nothing," Jack said, waving a hand which in the last seconds had been encased in an asbestos glove.

A *clunk* came from the bathroom. Elsie saw that the basin had tumbled from its pedestal. "Jack—you've been told to say it's nothing, I suppose!" Elsie was hoping only that he would tell the truth. Had they given him a pill?

The telephone rang.

Elsie ran down the stairs, rather surprised that the telephone was still working.

"Hello, *Elsie!*" said Jane. "You're still there? Aren't you leaving?"

Then came awful crackles on the line. "Where're you phoning from?"

"Eastern border of Golden Gate! Everyone's leaving! I'm so glad to get you because nearly all the lines are out! There's going to be an *earthquake!* Jack should know! Where is he?"

"He's here. He says they're trying to counterbomb it!"

"Elsie, dear, Golden Gate is . . ." *R-ZZZZ!*

The line went dead, really dead. What had she been about to say? Gone? Finished? At any instant Elsie thought the house would give a great heave and collapse—a death trap. *"Jack,"* Elsie yelled up the stairway.

Maybe he was still taking a look for things that might fall. She could hear the boys yelping with glee. Elsie lost patience, or couldn't think any more, and switched on the television. Channel 30 had no picture, just an excited voice saying, ". . . *not* try to fight the trees. We repeat the following important message: everyone is ordered to leave Golden Gate by copter if possible and at once. The roads are crowded—" A gasp betrayed the announcer's terror. "An earthquake of unusual proportions is believed imminent. We repeat, all . . ." Wails and squeaks silenced the voice, as if a giant hand had twisted up the station controls or throttled the announcer himself. There was a loud, dull thud from the empty screen—then nothing.

Elsie turned to see Jack standing just inside the living room doorway. He had heard it. His headgear was off now, and his face paler than before. Their sons flanked him, one bandaged, one not, but both had the jaded smiles, both were calm now though their sneakered feet were planted more apart than usual to keep their balance in the shaking house.

"All right, let's go," Jack said. "Let's get in the copters. No use trying to take stuff with us. We head east, okay, Elsie? East. Even if it's the desert. There'll be others. They'll bring food and stuff— from somewhere."

"All right, *yes*," Elsie said. "But why didn't you *tell* me—days ago? You *knew.*"

"C'mon, hon, no time for arguing," Jack said. "You kids hop, y'hear me? Head straight east, don't try to find us, just land where you see people. We'll get together later. C'mon, Elsie, let's *go!*" Jack trotted out after the boys.

A corner of the house collapsed, crushing the television and the sofa. Elsie walked out of her house. In the noise of distant sirens, explosions, she could not hear the hum of the boys' two copters, but she saw them rise and point east.

Jack's copter was in the driveway. "Get in your bus, hon! I started 'er for you!" He was standing with one foot on the copter step.

A tree fired at him—one of the poplars. Elsie saw the white jet shoot straight against the side of his head and fling him to the ground. Jack screamed. Another white bulge trembled as Elsie approached Jack, and at once she tiptoed, and bent low. Could the trees *see,* with a kind of radar?

Jack was trying to say something, but his jaw, half of it, had already been burnt away. He was dying, and there was nothing she could do. For a few seconds, Elsie endured a paralysis, clenched her teeth and looked upward, as if she expected some saving power to come from the heavens. She saw only a score of copters heading east, all flying unusually high.

"You all right, ma'am? Got a copter?" cried a voice behind her.

Elsie spun around and saw not far above her a copter with a rope ladder dangling, and the covered wagon device of the Forty-Niners on the side of the machine. A teenaged boy peered down from the driver's seat, friendly, smiling, anxious. Elsie said, "Yes, thanks. I'm just taking off."

"Can you manage him?" the boy asked quickly.

"He's dead."

The boy nodded. "Better hurry, ma'am." He floated off.

There was a rumble from the north like a huge wind, and a sound of splitting—and this came closer. Underground explosions? Or the earthquake? To the north Elsie saw vast woods and orchards tip slightly to the left. Elsie moved nearer her gates.

A crack was coming towards her like a live thing. She could see fresh brown and yellow earth to a depth of one hundred feet in the widening gorge whose point advanced by leaps. The earth left of the gorge had all been lifted, but was now tilting to the left. The crack veered to the right of her property. She could still dash to her copter and make it, she realized—just. But she didn't want to make it. What she witnessed seemed heroic, and right. A quick, fleeting thought of Jack came to her: *He treated me just like the public, as if I were just—*

Elsie turned to face the oak tree, *her* beloved young oak, which now quivered, pointing its crinkled white breast at her, as if gathering itself for its fatal spit. Elsie did not take her eyes from its pink center. Seconds passed, but it did not shoot.

The roar now was like that of a surf, and Elsie knew it was the sound of Golden Gate falling into the Pacific Ocean. Her house and land would go with it. Elsie clung to her iron gates, which themselves had tilted. Behind her and to her right, the oak shot its fiery sap, and bushes on her left burst slowly into flame. Elsie was glad the oak had fired before it drowned.

It was right, Elsie felt, right to go like this, conquered by the trees and by nature. How kind of the Forty-Niners—she thought as the iron bars jerked in her hands, bloodying her palms—to take a look at Rainbow, a district she knew the Forty-Niners hated because so many nuclear workers lived in it, just to see if they could be of assistance.

Now the wind whistled in her ears, and she was falling at great speed. A land mass, big as a continent, it seemed, big as she could see, was dropping—slowly for land but fast for her—into the dark blue waters.

About the Author

Born in Forth Worth, Texas, in 1921, Patricia Highsmith spent much of her adult life in Switzerland and France. She was educated at Barnard College, where she studied English, Latin, and Greek. Her first novel, *Strangers on a Train*, published initially in 1950, proved to be a major commercial success and was filmed by Alfred Hitchcock. Despite this early recognition, Highsmith was unappreciated in the United States for the entire length of her career.

Writing under the pseudonym of Claire Morgan, she then published *The Price of Salt* in 1953, which had been turned down by her previous American publisher because of its frank exploration of homosexual themes. Her most popular literary creation was Tom Ripley, the dapper sociopath who first debuted in her 1955 novel, *The Talented Mr. Ripley*. She followed with four other Ripley novels. Posthumously made into a major motion picture, *The Talented Mr. Ripley* has helped bring about a renewed appreciation of Highsmith's work in the United States as has the posthumous publication of *The Selected Stories*, which received widespread acclaim when it was published by W. W. Norton & Company in 2001.

The author of more than twenty books, Highsmith has won the O. Henry Memorial Award, the Edgar Allan Poe Award, Le Grand Prix de Littérature Policière, and the Award of the Crime Writers' Association of Great Britain. She died in Switzerland on February 4, 1995, and her literary archives are maintained in Berne.

AN